DARK TREE SHINING

PAULA HARRISON

nosy crow

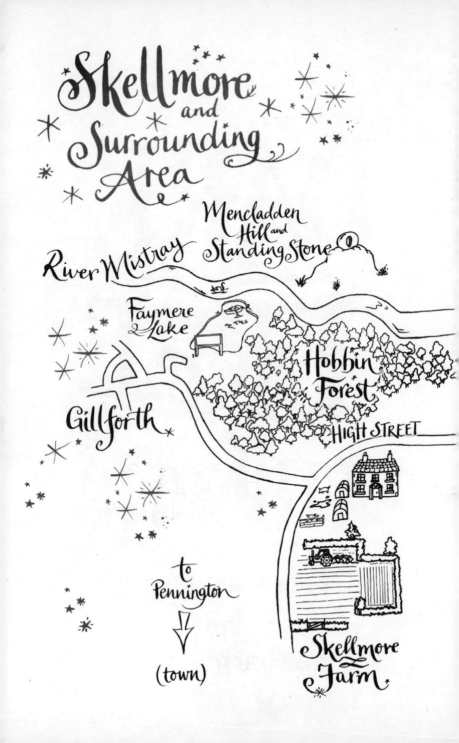

For Megan, who sees the magic in things

First published in the UK in 2013 as Faerie Tribes: The Wildwood Arrow
by Nosy Crow Ltd
The Crow's Nest, 10a Lant Street
London, SE1 1QR, UK

This edition published in 2015

Text © Paula Harrison, 2013
Cover illustration © Lisa Evans, 2015
Map and cover lettering © Sarah J Coleman, 2013, 2015

Printed and bound in the UK by Clays Ltd, St Ives Plc
Typeset by Tiger Media, Bishops Stortford, Hertfordshire

Papers used by Nosy Crow are made from wood grown in
sustainable forests.

ISBN: 978 0 85763 495 5

www.nosycrow.com

Prologue

Ten years before

The fire burned bright. It reflected in the little girl's eyes and cast a glow across her face. She crouched on the rug with her thumb in her mouth, watching the flames dance.

A woman in a red dress hurried over and wrapped a blanket round her, whispering, "Be really quiet for me, baby."

Then she snatched up the child and ran out into the darkness. Shadows moved in the air, circling the roof of the house. There was a faint swoosh before the night broke into splinters of lightning and the little girl hid her face.

The woman kept running until she reached the river. Then she took away the blanket and slid the child gently into the water.

"I love you, Laney," she told her daughter. "You'll be safe here. Daddy will find you."

The child smiled and water drops sparkled on her eyelashes. She sank under the surface, still smiling, *with her hair and dress floating out around her. She knew her mummy was right. She was safe here.*

The water felt like home.

CHAPTER

1

A small drop of water hung on the end of the kitchen tap, shimmering like a liquid diamond. Laney reached over the sink and let it trickle on to her finger. It balanced there, perfectly round and cold against her skin. Her heart beat a little faster and she knew right then that she had to try out her faerie power again.

"Are you daydreaming, Laney?" Kim, her stepmum, bustled over with the breakfast bowls and mugs and stacked them up next to the sink. Laney's little stepbrother, Toby, galloped in with his arms spread out like an aeroplane and circled round her legs.

"Slow down, Toby!" said Kim, smiling. "No flying in the kitchen!"

"Me be Laney!" Toby gabbled.

"You're being Laney?" Kim looked puzzled.

"Woooo!" Toby ran twice round the kitchen table and then back to the sitting room, his arms still out wide.

Laney hid a smile. Toby had once seen her fly when she'd been in faerie form. Luckily no one was about to believe a two-year-old. She let the water drop fall off her finger. "Maybe he needs a good run around. You could take him to the park right now. I don't mind staying here and doing the washing up."

"Thank you, honey. That's really kind." Kim placed a light hand on Laney's shoulder. "Toby!

4

Where are your shoes?"

After a few minutes of rushing about and shoe-finding, the front door closed and the house was silent. Laney turned back to the sink. She could have tried this in the bathroom upstairs, but the basin was small and last time there had been a lot of spray. Her dad had guessed what she'd been up to and told her not to try out her powers in the house – though not to try them out at all was what he really meant. He ought to understand. He was a Mist faerie himself, no doubt using his power over water in his job as a plumber. The magic ran in families, so why didn't he see that she needed to practise her new-found skills, to learn to control them?

The sun came out from behind a cloud and shone through the window. Laney glanced at the clock. She had fifteen minutes till she had to meet Fletcher and Claudia by the river. Pressing her lips tight, she twisted the tap just enough to let out a thin trickle of water.

She would start with something small like making the water spurt sideways for a moment. Something easy.

She stared at the line of water. *Go sideways. Just for a second.*

The water carried on falling in a straight line and Laney felt a bubbling frustration. She could do this.

She knew she could. All Mist faeries could make water move. She stared harder. *Come on – do it now. Go left.*

Still nothing happened. Frowning, Laney put her hand under the cold water, letting it spill through her fingers. The water grew suddenly hot and tumbled faster and faster from the tap. She thought she heard the stairs creak. Wasn't her dad out? Her eyes flew to the window, looking for her dad's van, but it wasn't parked in its usual spot in the lane. She was sure he'd gone to work.

Steam rose from the falling water and the tap began to judder. Hot water spurted over the worktop and the breakfast bowls, and then right across the window. Laney grabbed for the tap and turned off the flow. Sunlight glittered through the water drops on the window as they made dozens of zigzagging watery paths down the glass. Her T-shirt was splattered with water too. She couldn't believe it had gone wrong. It was the same every time. First nothing would happen and then the water would go wild. She wiped her forehead, which was damp with spray.

The kitchen door opened. Laney's stomach lurched but she met her dad's look defiantly. There were gold circles around the pupils of his eyes, just like hers. Gold-ringed eyes were the mark of a faerie – a mark that only other faeries could see.

He surveyed the room, a serious expression on his face, and then he came in and shut the door behind him. "Laney?" he said quietly. "Why is everything wet?"

Laney blinked, suddenly thinking of faerie folklore. Why couldn't things be like the old days, before faeries lived with humans? In those days she would have been free to work magic, instead of having to hide her powers and pretend to be human.

She turned away from her dad's gaze. "I was just . . . I told Kim I'd wash up for her." She seized a tea towel and started mopping the worktop and the window.

"I've told you already – you can't behave like being a Mist faerie is one big experiment. You're drenching the place! You've got to stop."

"Fine." Laney shoved the plug into the sink and switched on the tap, squirting in too much washing-up liquid and filling the sink with bubbles.

"Are you actually listening to me? You can't use your powers just because you feel like it. Life isn't like that. We live in secret and people mustn't find out about us. Think of the consequences of your actions."

"Fine!" Laney grabbed a mug and washed it fiercely. She glanced at the clock again. Ten minutes till she had to meet Fletcher and Claudia.

Her dad caught the look. "Are you seeing Fletcher and Claudia again today?"

Laney put the mug upside down to dry. "Probably. It's still the summer holiday. *My* summer holiday."

"I know it is." Her dad stepped closer. "But listen, you've got to be more careful about being seen together. Peter Stingwood told me yesterday that he thought you were spending too much time with Fletcher. He said that you'd better not get in the way of the Thorns, whatever that means. Everyone's been so jumpy since the flood and now the tribes trust each other less than ever."

Laney thumped another clean mug on to the side. *The tribes.* It was always the tribes. Three different faerie tribes lived in the village of Skellmore. The Thorns, Greytails and Mists had very different powers and they didn't exactly make an effort to get along. Stingwood was a Thorn Elder who had never liked her. The warm water grew hotter beneath her fingers.

There was no way she was going to stop seeing Fletcher and Claudia, but she couldn't tell her dad that. They were hunting for the Myricals – five faerie objects of great power, each one sacred to a different tribe. They'd been searching for them ever since the Myrical belonging to the Mist tribe – the Crystal Mirror – had caused a flood that had nearly washed the whole of Skellmore away. But the hunt for the Myricals was a secret and it had to stay that way, because the evil Shadow Faerie was looking for them too. . .

The water fizzed around her hands and she jumped.

"Laney, just look at what you're doing!" Mr Rivers exclaimed. "It's as if you don't even realise you're using your powers half the time. You have to keep a clear head – don't lose control."

"Let me learn how to use my skills properly then!" Laney burst out. "You promised you'd talk to the Mist Elder about me going to training. I can't even *be* a proper member of the tribe unless I've done that."

Her dad sighed. "The Mists didn't even choose their new Elder till last week and things still haven't settled down properly. I just don't think it's a good time for you to get involved."

"But when *will* you ask? It's bad enough that my powers Awakened so late and everyone treats me like a freak!" Laney's voice rose. "Just because *you* don't want anything to do with the tribes—" She broke off, seeing from his face that she'd gone too far.

"Don't talk to me like that." His face stiffened and he folded his arms. "There's a lot you don't understand. You have no idea what the tribes are capable of. That's why I'm warning you about being seen with Fletcher and Claudia."

"We're just hanging out. There's nothing wrong with that, is there?" Laney washed the last plate and yanked the plug out. It was time to go. Claudia and Fletcher would be waiting.

"That's not how some of the faeries will see it."

Laney pulled down the handle of the back door. "I'll be back by teatime."

"Laney. . ."

"Don't stress. I'll be careful." She swung the door open before her dad could say any more and headed down the side alley into the narrow lane. One side of Oldwing Rise was lined by a quiet row of cottages. A thick wall strewn with ivy ran along the other side and marked the edge of the churchyard. Beyond the wall was the grey stone church of St Dunstan with its pointed steeple soaring into a boundless blue sky.

Laney crossed the lane and let herself into the churchyard, taking her usual shortcut round the side of the church. She knew a rippling light would be playing across the walls of her house behind her, like sunshine dancing on the sea. It was a sign, visible only to other faeries, that Mist faeries lived there. But she didn't look back. A simmering feeling built up inside her. Why couldn't she get the tap water to do what she wanted?

Her throat tightened. Most faeries Awakened

into their powers when they were quite young, but her Awakening had only been six weeks ago, on her twelfth birthday. Since then, she hadn't managed to prove her powers at all. In fact, everything she did seemed to convince everyone that she was useless. Maybe her dad didn't believe she could be a proper Mist faerie either and that was why he hadn't bothered asking Frogley, the new Elder, to train her. Maybe he was just trying to save her from disappointment.

The only good thing had been finding the Crystal Mirror. She'd held it, feeling it overflow with Mist magic. For weeks she'd thought about that feeling and now she was determined to show everyone that she had a lot more power than they knew.

CHAPTER 2

Laney's middle finger prickled and she rubbed it thoughtfully as she walked through the churchyard. She still had a red mark from when she'd burned herself on a candle weeks ago. It tingled sometimes, especially when her hands felt hot.

Clouds covered the sun, casting the churchyard into gloom. Laney followed the path round the corner past tilted gravestones. She could still see traces of the flood here and there – the dark line near the bottom of the church wall where the water had reached. She shouldn't be spending so much time on her own worries when there were Myricals to find. She sped up, until she heard voices and saw Craig Mottle and Jack Turney – human boys she knew from school.

They were coming out of the minimart with plastic bags and sniggering at something. Laney watched them swagger down the High Street. Craig got a fizzy drink out of his bag and took a long swig before giving a huge belch. Both boys sniggered again.

As they passed the Lionhart Pet Shop a pair of gigantic green cat's eyes on the wall blinked and a long growl made the ground tremble. Laney smiled to herself. Craig couldn't hear the growl. He couldn't see the huge cat's eyes on the pet-shop wall even though he walked past them every day. He couldn't see the shimmering white-pink cloud of sprites flying over the park or the mysterious shape of the faerie ring near the old oak tree. The whole village was full of magic signs that humans couldn't see. Laney remembered the first time she'd walked along the High Street after her eyes had gained their gold-ringed enchantment and she had seen her ordinary-looking village as it really was, with faerie power washing over the streets.

Laney reached the churchyard gate that led out on to the High Street. She thought she'd managed to slip by unnoticed until she heard Craig's voice.

"Ooh, it's Laney Rivers!" He blocked her path, stopping Laney from getting through the gateway. Jack Turney stood behind him, grinning.

"Can you move, please?" Laney glared at Craig. Of all the boys from school, Craig topped the list of the most annoying.

He grinned before taking another swig of his drink. "Make me!"

"Move, Craig!" Laney felt the frustration build up inside her – about her dad, about her powers that wouldn't work and the Mist training she wasn't getting. She glared at Craig's freckled face and his bottle. The feeling boiled higher, and suddenly a stream of fizzy orange shot right up Craig's nose.

"Ugh!" Craig stumbled backwards, orange liquid dribbling over his cheeks and chin on to his clothes.

"Oh, man! That wasn't cool," said Jack Turney.

"Look at your T-shirt."

Laney dashed past them and took the path that led to the river. She grinned to herself. It wasn't just that it served Craig right. Finally she'd managed to get some liquid to obey her command. Maybe her powers weren't totally useless after all!

By the end of the afternoon, Laney's arm was aching. She raised the small grey stone to her eye for the thousandth time and looked through the hole in the middle. All she could see was sheep and grass. Keeping the stone to her eye, she slowly checked the rest of the field, looking for any shimmering patches on the grass or in the air. These were spell vibrations and spotting them might lead to the discovery of a Myrical.

Behind Laney, Fletcher Thornbeam stood waiting, his hands in his jeans pockets and his face as still as rock. Claudia Lionhart was perched on top of the fence with her legs curled beneath her and Dizzy, her thin black cat, by her side. Laney knew her dad was right. There would be trouble if their tribes saw the three of them spending so much time together.

Claudia yawned. "Are we done yet? Seriously! Myrical hunting is exhausting and we've been searching all day."

"Nearly done!" Laney cast her eye across the

furthest part of the meadow. More sheep grazing on more grass, and a rusty bucket in one corner – that was it. She lowered the stone with the now familiar lurch of disappointment. Six weeks of this. Six weeks of nothing.

She turned, meeting her friends' gold-ringed eyes. "There's nothing here," she told them.

Fletcher pulled out a map, unfolded it and scribbled a note on it. "That's OK. We can tick this place off and move on."

Claudia sprang smoothly down from the fence and Dizzy leapt after her. "We should skip these other fields. They're all the same."

"We can't," said Fletcher. "We need to check them, just in case."

"It would be a lot quicker if we could change to faerie form," said Laney, thinking of the sudden rush of power that came with the change. "We could do a sort of fly over and check out each field that way."

"It might give the humans a bit of a shock," Fletcher said drily. "And we don't want people knowing what we're doing, remember?"

"I know – I wasn't really serious." Laney fidgeted. "It's just . . . getting annoying doing it like this." She didn't really mean annoying but she didn't know how to explain it. The simmering feeling had returned. If she didn't do something to relieve the pressure she felt like she might burst.

"We should mix things up by searching in town," said Claudia. "A change would be good."

"We can't just flit from one place to the next." Fletcher studied the map again, before folding it up. "We have to do this one bit at a time otherwise we'll miss somewhere out."

"Maybe we should split up and I'll cover town," said Claudia.

"I don't think the Myricals would be hidden in Pennington," said Laney. "It's not out of the way enough – what if a human found one of them or something?"

"I know we probably won't *find* anything in Pennington but at least we won't die of boredom. There are shoe shops!" Claudia's eyes glinted. "We'll be back at school in three days and I've hardly done any shopping this whole summer."

Fletcher raised an eyebrow. "Don't you think finding the Myricals is more important than buying shoes?" He clicked his fingers, making a tree branch swing aside, and then climbed the fence into the next field. Laney followed.

"Are we seriously expecting to find anything here though?" Claudia vaulted gracefully over the fence to join them. "The olden-day Elders hid the Myricals – the most powerful magical things in existence – and we expect to find them among the sheep dung?"

"They're just as likely to be here as anywhere else," said Fletcher stubbornly.

Laney's simmering feeling grew stronger. She wondered if it was the bickering between Fletcher and Claudia getting on her nerves. They fell out at least once a day, but as Fletcher was a Thorn and Claudia was a Greytail that was only to be expected. She pushed a wisp of hair away from her face. "I just wish we had some idea of where to look . . . a hint or something. I bet the Shadow faerie isn't searching like this. I bet he'll go straight to them!"

The sheep and bird calls sounded loud in the long silence. Claudia looked at Laney and then looked away again.

The words *Shadow faerie* hung between them all like a heavy cloud.

Fletcher broke the silence. "We haven't seen any sign of the Shadow for weeks and if Gwen doesn't know any more about where the Myricals are, then he probably doesn't either. He didn't know where the Crystal Mirror was, did he?"

"No, but I can't help wondering. . ." Laney tailed off. She felt she shouldn't mention the Shadow faerie, as if it might bring him here if she talked about him. A picture rose in her mind of that dark hood masking his face and his black wings stretching wide. . . She gulped. "I just can't help wondering where the Shadow is, that's all. He could be anywhere and no one else seems worried. No one saw him except us and Gwen, and the tribes never believed he existed in the first place."

"I know what you mean," said Claudia. "I keep wanting to warn the other Greytails. But Gwen told us to keep it a secret, especially as we don't know who the Shadow actually is."

"It's probably safer that way," Fletcher added. "There'd be fighting if people knew. There's already so much suspicion between the tribes. We just have to keep our mouths shut and carry on looking for the Myricals. It's the only way we can help."

"I guess so," said Laney. "But it feels like we're waiting for something bad to happen and it's getting on my nerves. I wish Gwen had some idea of where we should look."

Gwen Whitefern was the only tribe Elder that Laney trusted and the only one who knew about their search for the Myricals. She had explained how the sacred objects came to be – telling them that years ago each of the tribes had crafted a precious thing and poured the essence of their powers inside it. These were the five Myricals. The Mist tribe with its water magic had made the Crystal Mirror. The Thorns with their power over plants and trees had created the Wildwood Arrow. The Blaze tribe had put their power over fire into the Sparkstone, while the Kestrels had filled the Vial of the Four Winds with their power over air. Finally, the White Wolf Statue was made by the Greytails and they poured their powerful bond with animals into it.

Gwen had also told them how a great evil force had risen among the faeries, and how the tribes had planned to hide all the Myricals, only retrieving them when the evil was defeated. But by then the Myricals had been lost completely. Now a new evil was searching for the objects. And if the Shadow faerie took possession of one. . . Laney shivered. You could destroy masses of people and whole stretches of land with power like that. At least they'd made sure that the Crystal Mirror was safe. Passing it through the ancient Mencladden Stone outside the village at sunrise had locked it away inside Time itself.

Fletcher took the adder stone from Laney and used it to check the new field. "I can't see anything here either."

"Big surprise!" said Claudia. "It's just another field."

Fletcher ignored the comment and checked the field one more time. Laney noticed that Dizzy was standing stock still, her back arched and her black fur bristling. Then she uttered a long string of meows before rushing off into the undergrowth. Claudia, who had bent down to listen, straightened up and looked at Laney with raised eyebrows.

"What is it?" Laney knew cats were one of the few creatures that could see faerie magic and Dizzy was definitely spooked by something.

"Dizzy's caught the scent of someone crossing the river – a man from the Mist tribe."

"Do you think he knows we're here?" said Laney.

"He probably doesn't," Fletcher said quietly. "You go and see what he's doing, Laney – he's from your tribe. We'll stay hidden."

Laney went down the footpath that led to the riverbank. A tall, thin man with angular shoulders stood on the bridge that spanned the Mistray river. He was leaning on the railing, peering at the water over the top of his half-moon spectacles. Laney recognised him as Lucas Frogley, the new Mist Elder. He came from the neighbouring village of Gillforth, so she didn't know much about him.

Curious, Laney went closer to the river's edge, trying to work out why he was staring at the water so hard. A small whirlpool spun in the centre of the river directly below the bridge. Laney's eyes flicked from the man to the swirling water, sure he was creating it even though he gave no sign he was using his power. A bunch of leaves and sticks floating down the river were sucked into the whirlpool and vanished completely. Laney shivered.

"Ahh!" said Frogley, a smile widening on his pale,

bony face as he saw her. His stare made Laney feel as if she was something slimy he'd found on the riverbank. "Are you Elaine Rivers?"

"Yes, I'm Laney." She noticed the curling silver marks on the backs of his hands. Those were the marks of an Elder.

"Your father came to speak with me today," Mr Frogley said grandly. "Is it true that you Awakened quite recently?"

Laney nodded, hoping he wouldn't ask too much about that.

"Well, young lady!" He peered at her over his half-moon spectacles. "Your dad said you were keen to join us so I came to deliver the good news myself. You're invited to join our next Mist training session, just as long as you can guarantee one thing."

Laney smiled nervously. "Yes . . . sir?"

He leaned a little closer. "I want to be sure that you won't be spreading any more nonsense about a *Shadow*." He paused as if waiting for a reaction. "I'm certain it must have been that Whitefern woman filling your head with Thorn ideas and by now you must know that it was no more than a ridiculous lie. Hmm?"

Laney thought fast. "I won't mention anything about it." At least she could promise that without being untruthful – after all, they were supposed to be keeping what they knew a secret for now.

"Good." Frogley's mouth stretched into a wide smirk. "Because we can't welcome anyone whose words or actions will make a joke of our tribe, can we? The next training session is today, in fact, at Faymere Lake at seven o'clock. Don't fly there, don't be late and make sure that you're not seen on the way."

"Thank you. I will. I mean I won't," said Laney.

Frogley smiled again and his round eyes examined her closely before he turned in the direction of Skellmore.

Laney gazed at the water rushing under the bridge, her stomach flipping over. She couldn't believe it – she had thought her dad was never going to talk to the Mist Elder about her training. She had been wishing so hard for this, but what if she went along and did everything wrong?

Dizzy ran on to the bridge and sniffed the air, her tail held high, and Claudia and Fletcher emerged from the hedgerow on the riverbank.

"Did you hear all that?" asked Laney.

"Most of it." Claudia smoothed back her dark hair. "Greytail super senses, you see! So you're off to your first training session at last!"

Laney's stomach flipped over again. "Yeah. At last." She checked her watch. "Actually, I'd better get back."

"See you later." Fletcher smiled. "And good luck."

Laney slipped out of the house after tea. Her dad was out on a plumbing job. She'd wanted to thank him for getting her the invitation to the training session but at the same time she was glad he wasn't around. Her stomach was churning and she didn't think she could bear any last-minute advice.

She crossed the High Street, quickening her pace. A shimmering flock of sprites swooped down, making empty sweet wrappers skitter along the pavement. She breathed in, trying to get her heart to slow down.

She was worried about what the other Mists would say when she turned up at training, as the strange circumstances of the night she Awakened had made many faeries suspicious of her. It had been her birthday and hanging in the sky had been a Wolf Moon – a blood-red full moon, the worst omen in the faerie world. It had all led to the Elders performing the painful Seeing Thread test to check her power. She pushed the memory of it away. She had to concentrate on tonight.

The sun dipped in the sky and her pulse began to race again. She needed to get moving. She only had twenty minutes to get round the edge of Hobbin Forest to where they were meeting, and she'd been told that she mustn't fly. The risk of a human seeing her was too great if she used her wings before dark.

Her phone beeped. It was a message from Steph, her best friend, who lived in town.

It had been hard knowing what to say to Steph lately. Steph was human, so she couldn't be told a single thing about what Laney had been going through all summer. Feeling bad, Laney pocketed the phone again. She'd have to talk to her later.

Crossing the High Street, she walked through the yard behind the minimart that was full of recycling bins and empty packing crates. Then she climbed over the fence into the field behind the shop. Hobbin Forest lay on the opposite side of the meadow, a dark mass of trees with the burnt-orange sun hovering above them. Breaking into a run, she followed the path to the edge of the trees. The path ran along the side of Hobbin Forest for a couple of miles.

Hurrying through the deepening dusk, Laney thought of the Shadow faerie and shivered. What if he was in Hobbin Forest right now? She glanced at the trees to her right. For a second, she wished Claudia and Fletcher were with her. Then she reminded herself that she couldn't turn up to her first Mist training with a Thorn and a Greytail.

She'd thought that the terror of meeting the Shadow would start to fade, but there were times when his cold laugh still echoed inside her head. Before the flood he'd invaded her dreams and, even when that nightmare ended, nowhere felt completely safe.

Branches creaked above her and great black wings spread wide. Laney gasped and stumbled. She recovered her balance and stared at the black crow, flapping off through the treetops. She had to get a grip on herself.

She stepped over a patch of brambles and carried on, trying to shake off the feeling of being watched. The path grew stonier and her feet ached. Thinking she heard voices, she stopped and peered through the half-light to see if there were any other Mist kids ahead of her.

A faint rustling came from the ground and something crept over her trainer. She glanced down and noticed a long twig lying across her foot. Shaking it off, she took a few more steps before she felt something coil itself around her ankle. She reached down and unhooked the knobbly stem that snaked away across the ground.

Suddenly she realised it was a tree root. It had a thin gnarled look about it from a lifetime spent underground. Why wasn't it buried deep in the earth? Then, from the corner of her eye, she saw movement. She lifted her head and froze.

A towering figure dressed in a long black cloak and hood glided down the path towards her. In a heartbeat, Laney felt transported back to the moment she found the Crystal Mirror. She pictured the Shadow towering over her and sliding the Mirror easily from her helpless fingers.

She heard a shout and the figure on the path raised one black arm. Laney screamed and ran.

CHAPTER 3

Laney stumbled over bumps in the path, expecting at any moment to feel the burning pain of the Shadow's red lightning.

No lightning came.

She ran on, not daring to look back. Perhaps the Shadow had taken to the air? He could be about to land right in front of her, spreading out his monstrous bat-like wings.

Struggling for breath, she pounded down the footpath, hoping for a glimpse of Faymere Lake and the other Mist faeries. The ground grew stonier and she could see the glint of water in the distance. She fixed her eyes on the water and tried to gain speed.

She was nearly there, so close – but then her foot caught on something hard sticking out of the path and she fell. Her hands and knees smacked into the stony ground. The world spun over and as she lay gasping she heard someone laugh.

Stumbling up, she turned to look for the Shadow, her heart still hammering. She was right by the edge of the lake, in the centre of a group of kids, and a figure was walking down the path from the trees. He wore a long coat that flapped as he walked and the light from the setting sun shone on his face – a kind face with a broad nose framed by fuzzy dark hair.

There was no hood, no vast black wings. This wasn't the Shadow.

She brushed the dirt off her jeans, feeling stupid.

The man with the long coat walked straight over. "Are you all right?" he asked. "I thought you must be a Mist on your way to training and tried to catch up with you, but you ran off."

The kids whispered to each other and there was a sharp burst of laughter.

Laney flushed a deep red. She knew everyone was staring, dozens of gold-ringed eyes all fixed on her. "I was hurrying. I just didn't want to be late," she said lamely.

"It was a good way to make an entrance, if that's what you were aiming to do." Laney turned at the sound of Frogley's voice, and he frowned at her over his half-moon spectacles. "OK, everyone, are we all here now? This is Joe Fenworth. He's come to help us." He indicated the younger man with the long coat and thick, dark hair. "Gather round now and we'll start."

The kids crowded closer and Laney edged to the back. There was a mixture of younger and older kids, some from the villages of Gillforth and Pyton. She spotted Leah Millbrook with her shiny grey glasses and the tall figure of Cathy Rainer, who she knew from school. She hadn't known they were Mists, but it made sense somehow. A boy in front of her looked round and nudged the girl next to him, who glanced round too. Laney's heart sank when she saw who it was: Jessie Weir.

Jessie's eyes gleamed and she shook back her curly dark hair as she whispered to the boy. Then they both sniggered. Laney felt her cheeks turn red again. Jessie had always been the Queen of Mean and she hadn't expected anything else.

But now she was getting funny looks from Cathy and Leah too, even though they'd always been friendly before. She guessed that Jessie had done a good job of filling everyone in on her late Awakening.

Mr Frogley cupped his hands and breathed into them. Letting them open, he released a thick blue vapour that went swirling up into the air. The mist spread out, forming a barrier around the edge of the lake. Then he released several glowing white orbs that floated into the air, casting a pale light over the surroundings.

"We are cut off from human eyes for a while." Mr Frogley chuckled as he looked round at them. "Safe and sound, eh? All the same, there will be no flying during this session and you must get back home on foot. Better safe than sorry."

At this news, there was some grumbling from the older kids, but Frogley ignored it. "As you know, we've missed training for a few weeks, but now we must work on our skills more than ever. Some members of the other tribes blame us for the flood, even though we worked hard to stop it. We must stay strong against the other tribes. . ."

Laney stared at the lake as Frogley carried on talking. The surface of the water looked dark and enticing. Faymere was meant to be really deep. The thought of all that water made her want to dive in and use her water wings.

She touched her shoulders, thinking of what it felt like when her wings unfolded . . . that sudden swish as they spread out behind her and the feeling of freedom as she climbed into the air. Frogley hadn't told them to change into faerie form though, and she didn't want to mess up at her first training session. She dug her hands into the pockets of her jeans. She had to act normal – the same as any other Mist faerie. She tried to tune back into what Frogley was saying.

"Sevensies, you can go with Mr Fenworth. Flyers, you're with me. Divide up, please." He waved a bony arm, indicating that they should move.

Laney looked around, confused. What did he mean – Sevensies and Flyers? She wished she'd been listening properly.

Everyone around her shuffled into two groups; the older ones stood together while the younger ones moved to where Joe Fenworth was standing. Laney stood in the middle on her own. Feeling awkward, she edged towards the older ones. All the kids she recognised from school were in that group.

"You're with the Sevensies for now, Laney." Mr Frogley pointed at the younger group. "Better to start at the beginning, eh? Everyone has to learn to toddle before they can run."

There was a spurt of laughter from Jessie, and Laney flushed again. Leah and Cathy were smirking too, she noticed; in fact, most of the older group were grinning. She should have known she'd be put with the younger kids. She pushed tendrils of hair off her face and stood with the Sevensies, ignoring all the stares. Swinging his skinny arms, Frogley strode down to the water's edge and his group drifted after him.

"OK, everyone!" beamed Joe Fenworth. "As it's my first time helping here, I'd like someone to show me what you've been working on. Who wants to go first?"

The little kids started jumping up and down, their hands in the air. "Me! Me!" shouted a curly-haired boy at the front.

"OK, Sam," laughed Joe, "why don't you have a go then? Just take your time."

Laney hunched her shoulders, trying to disappear at the back of the group. How embarrassing to be with a bunch of kids who were barely up to her waist. The heavy feeling that had been bothering her all day grew stronger. It filled her body until every movement felt like a huge effort.

The curly-haired boy picked by Joe Fenworth walked over to the lake and the group followed. He closed his eyes and pointed his finger at the water with tight-lipped concentration.

Three large drops of water lifted from the lake's surface and rose into the air, catching the pale light from the glowing orbs as they turned. The boy opened his eyes. His face grew redder and his pointed finger trembled. Then he let go of his breath and the water fell back into the lake.

"That's great!" said Joe. "Next time see if you can breathe while you do it. We don't want you passing out every time you try to use your powers! OK, guys! Let's start with moving water drops like Sam did. Just a few small drops though – no drenching anybody!"

"That's too easy!" groaned a small girl with plaits. "Why can't we do something harder?"

"Well, if you're all amazing at that we'll move on to freezing water and making rain showers," Joe Fenworth told her. "All right, spread out, everyone!"

The kids spread out into a line along the edge of the lake with Laney on one end, feeling giraffe-sized next to the others.

The Sevensies began their exercise and a collection of water drops rose into the air. Laney watched them, unable to pull her gaze away. All the

Mist tribe children seemed oddly similar. Maybe it was the way they moved so smoothly or something about the ever-shifting thoughts behind their eyes. Something united them, and whatever it was she just didn't know if she had it too.

She saw Joe Fenworth coming over and realised she should be doing the water-moving exercise. Hurriedly she stared down at the lake, desperately hoping this wouldn't go wrong.

"Laney! First time, is it?" Joe gave her a kindly smile.

"Yes." Laney flushed again and tried changing the subject. "Why's this group called the Sevensies?"

"It's the lowest of the three levels of faerie skill. It's actually called the Moon Learners. When you know a bit more you'll move into the Moon Flyers. The very top level is the Mystics but you have to be able to do pretty awesome things to reach that stage." He nodded towards the Mist Elder. "Mr Frogley is a Mystic."

"But why did he call this group Sevensies if it's actually the Moon Learners?"

Joe Fenworth coughed. "Um . . . it's a nickname that began because most of the kids in the group are about seven years old."

"Oh." Laney's shoulders sank.

"So, anyway! Let's make a start. Show me what you can do."

Laney stared at the lake, willing a water drop to rise out of it. The water rippled but nothing else happened. She rubbed the burn mark on the end of her middle finger.

"Just relax, Laney!" urged Joe. "Let your mind connect with the water."

The other Sevensies had gathered round them now, watching Laney with curiosity. Laney stared at the water, but it didn't move. She wished the heavy feeling inside her would go away.

There was a shout from the Flyers group further along the shore. A shining column of water spurted high into the air and looped down in a perfect arc. Then another column rose and another. Laney bit her lip. Obviously the Flyers could manage something a bit more complicated than floating a few drops in the air.

"Concentrate, Laney! You won't be able to do it unless you clear your mind of distractions," said Joe.

"Sorry!" Laney turned back to the water. This time she managed to slip past the heavy feeling and her mind drifted to the lake. She sensed the sway of the water – how it flowed and moved with each tiny droplet acting as one. She sought out a water drop and lifted it, willing it into the air.

It wouldn't go. It slipped from her grasp and trickled away.

Patiently she took another drop . . . but this one slipped away too.

A giggle broke through the shell of Laney's concentration.

"Shh, Sam!" said Joe. "Keep quiet."

The heavy feeling pushed at Laney and her hands grew hot. She wasn't going to be laughed at. She was going to make this water move right now. *Move!* she told it silently, and pointed at the lake. The water boiled at her feet like a cauldron, rolling and seething, until it exploded upwards and sent a fist of hot liquid straight down on their heads.

The Sevensies shrieked, water dripping from their clothes.

Laney watched the water drain back into the lake, surprised at the sudden drenching. Strangely, the heaviness inside her was gone and her mind felt clear. It was such a relief to be rid of the horrible, pent-up feeling – as if she'd climbed her way out of a small, dark cage.

Mr Frogley left his group. "What happened here? Who did this?" He looked at Laney.

"I was just trying to move one drop," she said.

"But look what you did!" Frogley's eyes glinted in his bony face. "This is monstrous . . . outrageous . . . to turn water into that!" Laney followed the jerk of his head. A patch of lake water had darkened and black lumps floated on the surface.

"If you were struggling to move a few water drops, then how did you manage to orchestrate this kind of catastrophe?" said the Mist Elder. "Making water boil is a high-level skill and cannot be learned without a great deal of practice."

"I really didn't do it on purpose. I'm sorry." Laney clasped her hands together. They were cooler now but the patch on her middle finger prickled. The lumps floating on the lake's surface looked like strange black rocks. Had she really made that happen?

Frogley stepped closer to Laney, his pale face furious. "You need to start explaining yourself, young lady. You were tested with the Seeing Thread when you Awoke – Miss Reed told me about it – and it showed that you had very little power."

Laney winced. The test had been painful. She didn't want to remember it.

"Perhaps Miss Reed reported it wrong," suggested Joe. "It's a pity we can't ask her about it but I think she planned to be away up north for a while."

"Visiting the north! She's sulking because she didn't get made tribe leader." Frogley rounded on Laney; his breath smelled sour.

"Well? Tell me the truth, girl. You've been Awake for several weeks so you must have some idea of your own capabilities. Was the test not done properly? Is it not true that it revealed you have very little power?"

Laney folded her arms. For weeks she'd barely been able to move a water drop but she wasn't going to admit that to him. "I think I have as much power as anyone," she said.

CHAPTER 4

"Sit there and don't move." Frogley pointed to a flat boulder before he lumbered back to the older group. Joe followed him and the two men began talking in low voices.

Laney sat down on the rock and stared at the Sevensies, who had gone back to raising neat little rows of water drops from the lake. Further away along the shore, the older kids were producing small rain showers with a click of their fingers. Laney caught a tiny piece of Mr Frogley's conversation. ". . . it hardly seems possible . . . perhaps her powers are erratic . . ."

She knew what erratic meant. Her powers weren't to be trusted. One minute they were working and the next she couldn't do a single thing. She'd told Frogley that she thought she had just as much power as anyone. But what good was that if she couldn't control it?

Her throat tightened. The blue vapour barrier was thinning and she could see the edge of Hobbin Forest over her shoulder. She stared at the trees. She couldn't shake off a feeling that something was watching her.

Training ended and the kids trudged away in small groups towards their villages. Jessie cast Laney a mocking look as she left, and Cathy and Leah didn't look at her at all. She hung back, wishing she had the guts to speak to them and try and explain.

A breeze lifted her hair and she suddenly realised that everyone else was a long way ahead. The darkness thickened. She wanted to be brave but the thought of walking all the way back along the edge of the forest by herself made her shiver. What if the tree root fastened round her ankle again? It was so dark that she wouldn't even see it coming.

She stood still for a moment, undecided. Mr Frogley had told them not to use their wings. On the other hand, she'd already messed up her first Mist training so did it really matter what he thought? Defiantly, she willed herself into her faerie form. Her human body dissolved in an instant, leaving behind her faerie shape, gleaming with power.

She flexed the wings that unfolded from her back and rose into the air, nearly bumping her head on a branch. She smiled, thinking for a moment of all those humans who believed in tiny-sized fairies. What would they say if they could see her now – as tall as ever but with glowing skin and pale-blue wings?

Soaring into the sky, she veered away from the forest and flew over the fields. A half-moon lit the countryside below and she sped up, unable to resist swooping through the night air. To her left, she could see figures walking along the footpath. It had to be people on their way back from training. She grinned. Keen not to be spotted, she decided to take the long way round.

She landed in a field on the edge of Skellmore, closed her wings and changed back to human form. Then she trudged down the footpath into the yard behind the minimart, her head filled with the image of the boiling lake water. After weeks of dull Myrical hunting, something had finally happened. It just wasn't anything good.

"So how did it go, Water Girl?"

Two figures sat on the fence on the far side of the yard, slightly hidden by the overhanging branches of a tree. The nearest figure was Claudia, who sprang down from the fence in a smooth cat-like movement.

"I didn't see you!" said Laney.

"We decided to hide until you came along. The grown-ups are getting really edgy about kids from different tribes hanging out together. My mum told Tom off for chatting to a Mist this morning – as if my dear brother would ever change his Greytail ways!" Claudia grinned. "So we hid and he did some weird Thorn camouflage spell." She jerked her head at Fletcher, who ducked out from under the branch.

"Well, it worked, didn't it? So don't complain," he said.

"I'd rather skip it next time though." Claudia shuddered. "It was all slithery leaves and smelly herbs. I feel like I'm covered in prickles and scratches."

"Can Thorn faeries get tree roots to move?" asked Laney suddenly. "I saw this long root creeping around on the edge of the forest in a freaky way. I don't know what it was doing out of the earth."

"That's weird," said Fletcher. "Some Thorns can use root spells, but usually only if they're at Mystic level."

"Oh." Laney paused. "Find any Myricals after I left?"

Fletcher thrust his hands in his pockets. "Nope. We checked one more field but there was nothing hidden there."

"We think we should see if Gwen has another adder stone," said Claudia.

"You mean *you* think we should," Fletcher replied.

"That way we can split up and search faster," said Claudia.

Fletcher folded his arms. "That's if there even *is* another one."

Laney pushed her hair away from her face. Going to Gwen's house might give her a chance to ask her about what had happened at Mist training. She checked her watch. "It's not that late. Let's go and ask her now."

They checked that the High Street was empty before leaving the yard. The minimart, hairdresser's and pet shop were closed up and street lamps cast pools of orange light on to the road. In the park opposite, the dark shape of the huge oak tree swayed for a moment and a golden glow swept up its trunk.

Laney never got tired of seeing how the oak sucked power through its roots from the faerie ring nearby. The golden light rose up the tree, filling the trunk first and then every branch and leaf, until the whole tree shone. A moment later the glow was gone.

Faerie rings were common in the area, making it a place rich in power. Laney always kept her distance from them though. The singing voices inside the ring were enticing, but if you got too close to one you could be sucked into the Otherworld for ever.

As they crossed the road, a group of cats clustered by the park railings surrounded Claudia, weaving in and out of her legs and purring. Dizzy jumped up on to the railings and Claudia listened to her mews carefully. Fletcher edged away from a large black-and-white cat that was trying to rub against his ankle. "The longer we stand here, the more likely we are to be spotted – let's go."

"Just a sec." Claudia put her head to one side as she listened to Dizzy. "Hmm, that's all a bit worrying. Keep an eye on it, guys," she told the cats. "But don't get too close to anything dodgy."

The cats slipped away, disappearing into the

gloom in seconds.

"What did she say?" Laney asked.

"They've seen traces of weird spells in the forest," said Claudia. "It's probably nothing. Dizzy gets a bit spooked sometimes. I think she likes the thrill of it, actually."

At the end of the street Laney, Claudia and Fletcher turned into Gnarlwood Lane, where the Thorns lived. They passed the Willowby house on the corner with its rough walls like a tree trunk. Next to it was Gwen's house, all covered in ivy with five huge trumpet-shaped white flowers forming the roof. Laney ran up to the front door and knocked.

Gwen Whitefern opened the door, her short frame wrapped in a cloak and her thin white hair escaping from the edges of a soft green hat. A sense of peace settled over them, as if even the air was stilled by her gaze. "Good evening. What brings a Mist, a Thorn and a Greytail to my door at this hour?" She scanned their faces. "There's no news yet, I see."

"No, we haven't, you know, found anything," said Laney. "We just wanted to talk to you. I hope it's not too late at night." She always had the urge to bow to Gwen, but she stopped herself.

"No, it's not too late." Gwen's deep eyes scanned Laney's face again and she opened the door wider. "Come in."

Her sitting room, with its flowery sofa and smell of cookies, gave away nothing of Gwen's power. But the corridor that led to the plant house was lined with criss-crossing vines that climbed the walls and clung to the ceiling. Lit with an emerald glow, the plant house with its glass walls and roof was brimming with trees and flowers. Laney wondered where the light was coming from and saw a plant with luminous, sword-shaped leaves in the centre of the little jungle.

Gwen made her way slowly to a garden bench and as she sat down a rose bush leaned closer and burst into flower. Gwen was a Thorn Elder, and by now Laney was used to the way plants behaved around her, drawn out by the strength of her magic.

"I'm afraid I can't talk for long," Gwen told them. "I'm going out to gather herbs tonight and I must leave soon. What is it you wish to speak about?"

"We've been using the adder stone like you told us," said Fletcher. "But it's taking such a long time. Maybe if we had a second stone, or even one each, we'd be able to search quicker." He took the stone from his pocket.

Gwen reached for it – deep lines etched across her face. Still holding the adder stone, she rose and tottered up and down the plant house. The flowers' heads turned, following her movements. "At least the Crystal Mirror is safe," she muttered. "That one is safe for now."

Laney wasn't sure whether to interrupt. "So we wondered if you had another adder stone we can borrow?"

Gwen handed Fletcher the stone and turned back along the passageway. "Come! I must check my remedy before I go out."

Laney, Claudia and Fletcher exchanged looks. "Do you think something's up?" said Claudia.

"I'm not sure," Laney whispered, and followed the Thorn Elder down the passageway.

Gwen stopped in the kitchen, where a large copper saucepan stood on the stove with purple liquid bubbling inside it, giving off a sharp smell like pine leaves. Gwen stirred the mixture with a wooden spoon. "You want another adder stone," she said.

"Yes, to help us find the Myricals faster," said Laney.

Gwen fixed her tawny eyes on them and the silver marks of an Elder shone on the backs of her wrinkled hands. "Do not be in such a hurry. It's better for you to search slowly and search together, and if you discover something, come and find me. And if you see any signs of the Shadow, keep well away from him. As yet we do not know what his next move will be."

Laney stared at the bubbling purple liquid in the

copper saucepan, a picture of the Shadow rising in her mind – the vast wings, the stench of decay. . . Every time she remembered, it felt as if a hand was squeezing her heart. She tried to push the image out of her head.

Claudia picked up a tall jar standing on the side and gave it a shake. The metal padlock on its lid rattled.

"Claudia! Put that down, please!" Gwen commanded. "I did not give you permission to pick anything up."

"Sorry!" Claudia stared curiously into the jar as she put it back. "What's in there? It just looks like dried ferns."

"It's moonwort – usually a harmless kind of plant – but this specimen is different and its effect could be extremely perilous. In fact, it's the strongest herb I have." She eyed Claudia sternly before turning back to the copper pan and murmuring, "This needs much more attention. Time for a little help, I think."

She picked a shiny privet leaf from a potted plant on the worktop. Cupping it inside her hands, she whispered to it and let it fall to the floor.

Reaching the ground, the leaf began to multiply, building upwards one leaf after another. It formed a tall human-like figure, made completely from small leaves, with two arms and legs but no features. The leaf figure didn't move but Laney thought there was something unnerving about its eyeless face and Claudia sprang back, eyes widening.

"Whoa! I've never seen that before," said Fletcher.

"Keep stirring." Gwen passed the spoon to the leaf figure, which took it in its green hand and stiffly began to move it round and round. "I'd like you three to keep an eye on him for five minutes before you leave," she said to Laney, Fletcher and Claudia. "These leaf spells are usually quite reliable, but occasionally I make one who stirs too hard or not hard enough. Just watch him for a little while, please, and then he can continue on his own."

"Sure! We'll watch him," said Fletcher.

"Er . . . yeah!" Claudia looked doubtfully at the leaf man. "As long as there's just one of them. They can't multiply into an army, can they?"

Gwen didn't answer. Instead she walked into the front room where she picked up a large wicker basket. "Help yourselves to a glass of elixir from the fridge and let yourselves out when you're ready. I won't be back till morning." She straightened the hat on top of her white hair and closed the front door behind her.

Laney's shoulders sagged. She'd been too chicken to mention the disaster at Mist training. She'd hoped to get a quiet moment without Claudia and Fletcher listening, but Gwen had left so quickly.

"She seems strange today," said Claudia. "Do you reckon something's up or is it just a weird Thorn thing?"

Fletcher ignored that. "Maybe there's something on her mind, something that the Elders don't want us to know about." He opened the fridge and poured sparkling green elixir into three glasses. Laney took a sip and instantly felt more energetic. Gwen's elixir tasted like mint and berries, all mixed together with Thorn magic. It was a powerful combination.

"I bet the Elders keep lots of secrets from the rest of us." Claudia edged away from the leaf-man, eyeing him suspiciously. "Does that thing have ears? Do you think we can talk safely in front of it?"

Laney leaned round to look at the leaf-man's head. The blankness of it made her stomach turn over. "I don't think it has senses. It doesn't even have a face."

The leaf-man went on stirring in a steady rhythm. Steam curled up from the bubbling purple liquid, its transparent shape coiling as it rose into the air. It reminded Laney of something else that belonged to Gwen. "You know what? Gwen's got something that might help us."

"She didn't want to give us another adder stone," said Fletcher. "She wanted us to keep on searching together."

"I don't mean the adder stone," said Laney. "I'm talking about something that will show us where the Myricals were hidden in the first place."

CHAPTER
5

Laney crouched down and opened a cupboard by the leaf-man's knees, trying not to touch him. Close up she could see all the tiny leaves that made up his legs. They weren't even held together by anything and yet they moved as one as he bent forwards to stir the stuff inside the copper pan.

"What are you looking for?" said Claudia.

"Hold on." Laney peered into the darkness of the cupboard. Beside the sieves and saucepans was a brass weighing scale. The shelf above was filled with an odd collection of coloured bottles with faded, handwritten labels. She picked out a small, dark-blue bottle and held it up to show them. "I'm sure this is the right one. See! We can look at the Spirit Smoke!"

Gwen had used the Spirit Smoke six weeks ago to show the ancient story of the five faerie tribes and how they'd come to live among humans. Laney had no idea how it worked, but she'd thought of it a lot since then – the shapes and colours of the smoke had been so beautiful.

"Laney! We can't touch that," Fletcher told her. "Only the Elders ever use it. We don't even know what to do with it."

"How hard can it be?" said Claudia. "And if it can show the story of the first faeries, why can't it picture other times from our history too? We can ask it to display exactly where the Myricals were hidden. I think it's a brilliant idea."

"You would!" said Fletcher. "But if the Spirit Smoke had all the answers, don't you think Gwen would have used it already?"

Laney straightened up, frowning. "I still think we should try it. It can't hurt." She looked at the leaf-man, half afraid she'd see something on his blank face or sense a change in him to show that he'd heard what they were planning, but he just kept stirring steadily. Holding the bottle tight, she went into the plant house.

"It's a mad idea," said Fletcher, following her with Claudia. "What if Gwen comes back?"

"She said she wouldn't be back till morning, remember?" said Claudia. "Here, I'll hold it while you pull out the stopper." She took the bottle in both hands.

Laney's heart raced as a thin, grey smoke began to curl from the mouth of the bottle. It quivered in the green light of the plant house and then spread slowly outwards, filling the air with its haze. As it unfurled, it turned from grey to a mass of glowing colour.

Laney drew her breath in quickly. "What does Gwen do next?" she whispered to Claudia.

"I don't know! Try commanding it or asking a question," suggested Claudia.

The colours hung in the air ... glowing ... waiting.

Laney straightened her shoulders and tried to speak with confidence. "Take us to the time when the Elders hid the Myricals from the Great Shadow."

Slowly, the smoke gathered into shapes and lines, and a scene formed in the air. A scene of chaos. People ran in all directions. Parents snatched up their children. Wind tore through trees ripping branches from the trunks, while smoke billowed from the windows of a burning house. Then the sky darkened and people opened their mouths in soundless screams as a figure with black-edged wings descended, blasting white lightning from both hands.

Laney felt the hairs rise on the back of her neck. She didn't need to hear their cries to understand their fear. This had to be the Great Shadow – a faerie of immense evil who had terrorised the tribes before she was born. He was smaller than the Shadow faerie she'd met in her fight for the Crystal Mirror and he had blazing white eyes – blank at the centre with no dark pupils. Laney heard Claudia draw her breath in sharply. The terrifying, blank eyes came closer and closer, until Laney was afraid that the Great Shadow could see them – even through Time itself.

Then the smoke curled and shifted, changing the scene, and the white eyes vanished. A new scene gradually took shape. A group of adult faeries sat round a large table talking earnestly. Laney got the sense from their clothes and their manner that they belonged to different tribes.

"My dad told me that the Great Shadow rose thirteen years ago," Fletcher murmured. "Those must have been the Elders in charge at the time."

The smoke moved and the Elders got up from the table and left the room. One lady stayed behind. She crumpled a bright-yellow leaf and wove a spell in the air that spiralled outwards in expanding circles.

"That Thorn lady looks a little bit like Gwen," said Claudia, "except her hair is different."

The lady looked round warily and for a second Laney thought she'd heard them. Then she reminded herself that all this had happened before she was born. Everything she was watching was already frozen in Time.

The scene switched again – this time to a long avenue of silver birch trees. A tall man with a wild beard strode down the avenue. He carried a polished wooden arrow with a shining silver tip in both hands. The smoke pulled in sharply to show every detail of the arrow, from the feathers on the shaft to the shining arrowhead.

"That's the Wildwood Arrow!" Fletcher leaned forward. "I've seen it before in books but this is so clear."

Laney thought that the arrow – the Thorn Myrical – looked amazing. "He must be the Thorn Elder, going off to hide the arrow. See – I knew this would work!"

"Only a Thorn would grow a beard like that," said Claudia.

The tall man marched between the two long lines of silver birches. As he passed, each tree shot upwards, growing taller, greener and more alive.

"Look at how the arrow's changing the trees," said Laney. "It's like a ripple of energy. The power coming from it must have been huge – not even Gwen makes the plants grow like that."

The man swung round suddenly, as if hearing a noise behind him. Then all the smoke turned yellow and the picture disappeared.

"Where's it gone?" said Claudia. "It's like looking at a TV when the picture's gone fuzzy."

"We must be able to get the image back. I need to see the Arrow!" Fletcher moved in closer until his face was almost touching the vapour, but the smoke hung blankly in the air without moving.

"I thought you said this was a mad idea?" Laney said.

"I know I did, but the Arrow . . . it's the Thorn Myrical and it's got all of my tribe's power inside it. I just wanted to see it a bit more." Fletcher threw himself down on to the garden bench and a leafy vine curled consolingly along his shoulder.

Claudia prowled around the unmoving cloud of Spirit Smoke, looking at it from all angles. "Something's blocking it, like a jammed signal. I guess we'd better stop now." She uncorked the bottle again and held it up. The smoke curled downwards, sucked towards the deep-blue bottle like water to a plughole.

"Wait!" Fletcher got up from the bench and put his hand over the top of the bottle. "We should try to learn more about the Myricals themselves. Any extra information could help us with our search." He spoke to the smoke. "Go back hundreds of years and show us the Myricals from when they were made."

Straight away, the Spirit Smoke formed each shining Myrical in turn. Laney recognised the first as the Mist Myrical – the Crystal Mirror that shone like a thousand stars. She felt a flush of pride, remembering how she'd held it and felt the Mist power inside.

Next came the Sparkstone belonging to the Blaze tribe – a misshapen grey rock with a pitted surface. Laney couldn't help wondering why the tribe with power over fire had chosen a rock that looked so dull and lifeless. She stared at it, wondering.

After the Sparkstone came a slim-necked, transparent bottle. This was the Vial of the Four

Winds belonging to the Kestrel tribe. As Laney looked closer, she could see something moving ceaselessly inside the bottle and she wondered if it really was the heart of the four winds.

"The White Wolf!" Claudia exclaimed as a small animal figurine appeared. The pale statue showed the wolf tipping back its head in a howl, its eyes golden-ringed like a faerie's.

Lastly the Wildwood Arrow emerged from the shifting colours of the Spirit Smoke, its honey-coloured wood gleaming. Laney glanced at Fletcher, who was gazing raptly at it.

Then, one by one, each faerie tribe appeared, took their Myrical and gathered round it, filling it with magic so dazzling that Laney had to shade her eyes. The faeries held the objects aloft, each filled with the essence of their tribes.

"That must have been some spell," breathed Claudia. "Just look at them."

Laney knew what she meant. The faerie tribes, in their ragged medieval clothes, looked triumphant. Their joy shone across the Time gap of hundreds of years. It made her feel so sad that the Myricals had been lost and all that happiness had come to nothing.

She spoke to the Spirit Smoke. "Can you show us the Myrical that was hidden closest to Skellmore?" The smoke quivered and returned to swirling colour. Laney's shoulders sagged; perhaps it didn't know.

"Try changing the question," said Fletcher. "We could ask—" He was cut off by a loud noise from the kitchen that sounded like a saucepan falling on the floor.

"The leaf-man!" cried Claudia, and she and Fletcher sprinted out of the plant house.

Laney stayed by the Spirit Smoke. "Is he OK?" she called out to her friends.

"It's all right, he's just stopped working," Fletcher said from the other room. "It's like he suddenly forgot what he was supposed to be doing. So much for him working till morning."

Laney stared at the smoke, her mind spinning. There was one more thing she was desperate to know and she wanted to ask the Spirit Smoke without the others listening. After the way she'd made the lake water boil today, it seemed more important than ever.

She had to find out . . . not just if something was wrong. But if something was wrong *with her*.

She cleared her throat. "Why did I make the lake water boil at Mist training?"

CHAPTER

6

The Spirit Smoke formed a picture of Faymere Lake at sundown. Laney saw herself – a figure on the shore – and watched the water boil and the strange black lumps float to the surface. She squirmed, remembering that moment and the looks of the other Mist kids. But this wasn't telling her anything new.

A movement caught her eye as the smoke wove a different pattern into the scene. A red disc emerged slowly, as if it was coming out of the lake itself. Her eyes followed its crimson shape as it climbed into the night sky and kept on rising.

A blood-red full moon. The Wolf Moon that had appeared over Skellmore on the night of her Awakening.

For a second, she couldn't breathe. But the moon hadn't been that colour when she was at the lake for the training – it hadn't even been a full circle. How could the Spirit Smoke be so wrong?

Unless . . . maybe it was trying to tell her something else. Something about herself. She *had* just asked it why she'd made the water act so strange.

Laney vividly remembered the Wolf Moon glaring down that night as faerie enchantments had surged through her and her eyes had become golden-ringed for the first time. Many faeries were deeply suspicious of her because she'd Awakened under a red full moon. Such a moon was supposed to be a sign of terrible things to come.

There was an old faerie prophecy about someone born under a red moon who would cause chaos and disaster. The moon was not red the night of Laney's birth, but still the shame of that moon appearing when she Awakened seemed to follow her.

She glanced at the doorway. The others were still talking in the kitchen. There was time to ask another question without them hearing. She moistened her lips. She had to know what the connection was. What did the red moon have to do with her? "Show me the night I Awakened – the night of the Wolf Moon."

The smoke swirled. She saw her old self – a human with blue eyes, standing in her kitchen laughing with Kim and Toby. On the table was a birthday cake that spelled out her name in Smarties. She saw her dad come in, angry that they had lit the candles on the cake – he hated candles and matches, and would never allow them in the house. She watched herself blow out the candle flames with a sulky face. Then the picture shuddered and vanished as the smoke coiled itself up into a tightly shaped spiral. Faster and faster it twisted, climbing upwards until it had almost reached the glass roof. Then, with a burst of light, it exploded.

Laney was thrown backwards on to the hard tiled

floor of the plant house. She thought it was raining until she realised that bits of leaves, flowers and bark were showering over her.

"Laney?" Claudia was crouching beside her in seconds. "Are you OK? What was it? Did you ask it to show you a faerie battle or something?"

Laney let go of the bench she was gripping on to and touched her forehead. "Ow – my head."

"What did you *do*?" Fletcher gazed round the plant house in horror.

The plants had been bent over by the blast. Branches hung broken on some of the trees. Flowers lay crushed and the fallen leaves made a ripped green carpet across the floor. The Spirit Smoke had vanished leaving no wisps of colour behind in the air.

Laney got up, her head thumping. "What's Gwen going to say?"

"She's going to ask us why we trashed her house and why we took the Spirit Smoke without permission. I just hope she doesn't set a carnivorous plant on us. Where's the Spirit Smoke gone? I'd better put it away." Fletcher uncorked the blue bottle and scanned the air. "Laney – where is it?"

"I don't know. I think it's disappeared." Laney couldn't bear to look up at their faces. "I asked the Spirit Smoke to show me the night of the red moon. That's when it burst." Laney realised her hands were shaking. "Just showing me the night I Awakened blew it up. What does that say about me?"

"I don't believe in that red moon prophecy nonsense." Claudia swept the shredded leaves off the bench and sank down on to the seat. "None of us Greytails do."

Laney shook her head miserably. "Something happened at Mist training. I didn't want to tell you before."

"Go on. What is it?" said Claudia.

Laney swallowed. "We were practising raising drops of water from the lake and at first I found it really hard. I was worse than the other beginners and then . . . everything went wild. The water heated right up and started boiling. I'm not even supposed to be able to do something like that yet. Lucas Frogley was furious. What if I'm cursed somehow?"

"But in the prophecy, the person bringing bad luck is *born* on the night of a red moon and you weren't, were you?" said Fletcher.

Laney put her hands in her pockets. "No. And Dad showed the Elders my birth certificate too."

"Then don't worry. You probably just spoke to the Smoke in the wrong way. Or maybe it's not supposed to stay outside the bottle for so long." He touched a half-broken branch of a tree; the split healed up and the branch straightened again. "Let's clear this place up before Gwen gets back."

Claudia fetched some Thorn elixir from the kitchen and began watering random plants with it, while Fletcher walked around, touching damaged plants and whispering to them till they healed. Laney found a broom and swept up the fallen leaves. She dreaded what Gwen was going to say. These plants were so precious to her.

"That's better." Fletcher pushed back his dark fringe. "I'll just check the leaf-man in case he's forgotten what to do again."

But the leaf-man was still standing by the copper pan, stirring with the same steady rhythm.

They heard the chime of the church clock. It was midnight.

"The worst thing is, we still don't know anything more about where the Myricals might be hidden," said Claudia as they closed the front door behind them.

"I told you it wouldn't be that easy, or Gwen would have already done it," said Fletcher. "There's no quick way to find them. No quick spell or cheat's way out. We just have to keep going with the adder stone and mark each place on the map as we check it."

Claudia pulled a face behind Fletcher's back, making Laney smile faintly. "The mess was my fault," she said. "I'll come back in the morning and apologise to Gwen."

Fletcher pulled the adder stone out of his pocket and flipped it, letting it spin in the air before catching it again. "See you tomorrow."

Laney looked at her clock when she woke the next morning. The hands stood at quarter past seven. Usually, with only a couple of days left of the holidays, she'd be trying to have a lie in. But lately it seemed more and more important to spend every minute on the hunt for the Myricals.

She sat up, her mind running over everything that had happened the day before. The boiling lake water . . . the red moon in the Spirit Smoke. . .

She was sure she was missing something – a connection between them. The images circled inside her head like a movie playing in the wrong order. Shaking sleep away, she climbed out of bed and pulled on jeans and a T-shirt.

Delving in the bottom of her chest of drawers, she took out a pale-blue notebook. Kim had bought it for her as a diary a couple of Christmases ago, but she could never be bothered to write in it every day. She leafed through blank pages interspersed with the occasional scribble and stopped at the back page.

This was where she had written it down. This was

the prophecy of the red moon as expressed in faerie lore. She read it silently.

Born under a Wolf Moon, the Child of Aether joins together powers far apart. He binds the opposites and drives a splinter through the faerie ring's heart.

She needed to be completely sure that the prophecy had nothing to do with her. Running downstairs, she went straight to the computer in the corner of the sitting room. The new carpet, put in after the flood, cushioned her feet. Kim and her dad were talking in the kitchen. Toby galloped in wearing a Superman cape.

"Fly, Laney!" he yelled.

"Toby! Shh!" Laney leaned down to switch the computer on.

"Fly! Woo!" Toby ran round and round the sofa with his little cape billowing out behind him. As soon as he got close enough, Laney grabbed him and gave him a tickle to stop him yelling anything else about flying.

There was a knock at the back door and Laney heard Simon, her dad's workmate, come in.

"I'm nearly ready, Simon. Just got to put some things in the van," her dad called back as he walked through to pick up his jacket. "Oh, morning, love. I thought you'd be enjoying your last chance for a lie in."

"I couldn't sleep," said Laney. "Must be the

thought of going back to school."

Her dad lowered his voice. "Did you go to the training session yesterday? Was it all right?"

The Mist training was the last thing Laney wanted to talk about, but her dad was being so nice. "It was OK – you know. Thanks for asking Frogley if I could go."

Simon appeared, leaning against the doorframe and looking tall and gangly. "You're up bright and early, Laney."

"Hi, Simon." Laney smiled. Simon's eyes were gold-ringed like her dad's. She thought again what a perfect job plumbing was for two Mist faeries. Just then the computer screen loaded and she typed in her password.

"OK, I'll meet you there, Robert," Simon told Laney's dad. "Bye, Kim." He made his way out through the front door.

Laney angled the screen so that no one would see it unless they came right over. She typed in *wolf moon*, but it came up with very little. Then she tried *red moon*, which brought up a lot of images. She thought for a moment and typed *dates of red moons.*

Only one astronomy website listed the dates when red moons had been seen in the sky. Laney scanned the list for the year of her birth. There had been a red moon that year, but not in July when she was born.

She became aware of how quiet it was. Twisting round, she saw Toby on the floor playing with a plastic teapot. Voices came from the kitchen, but they were muffled. Laney got up and crept over to the doorway. Adults always made it so obvious when they were saying stuff they didn't want you to hear. The way they dropped down to a whispering tone was a dead giveaway.

"It wouldn't be that hard to move," Mr Rivers was saying. "It would be so much easier for me if we were living in town. Most of my jobs have been in Pennington lately so there'd be much less travelling. You'd be closer to the shops. Everything would be more convenient."

"Since when have I wanted to be closer to the shops?" Kim's voice rose in amusement. "We've been here for nearly seven years now. What's wrong with Skellmore all of a sudden?"

"Well, Laney's getting older now. There's more for her to do in town, and she wouldn't have to get the bus to school every day."

"She's made new friends here lately though. I don't want to take all that away from her." There was a pause and the sound of a cupboard closing. "You haven't fallen out with someone, have you? I know some of the people who live here are a bit strange – that Gwen Whitefern with all her odd hats. I often think there must be something funny in the water." Kim laughed.

A knot twisted in Laney's stomach. She knew why her dad wanted to move. He wanted to get her away from other Mist faeries, and from Claudia and Fletcher. He probably only got her invited to the Mist training so that she'd stop trying out her powers at home while all the time he planned to persuade Kim to move house. Then he could stop her from seeing Skellmore people altogether.

"No, I haven't argued with anyone. I just think it would be better for all of us if we lived in town." Mr Rivers' voice was almost too quiet to hear.

There were footsteps and Laney dashed back to the computer. She clicked off the screen with the dates of the red moons just as her dad came through and picked up his toolbox from the hallway.

"Toby! Breakfast time!" Kim called, and Toby galloped off to the kitchen.

After her dad had left, Laney switched off the computer. She knew her dad didn't trust the other faeries. He didn't even trust his own tribe, the Mists, but every faerie's power ran in their family and there was nothing he could do about passing it on to her. Sometimes she wondered if Toby would turn out to have powers when he was older too. Kim was human but maybe only one parent had to be a faerie for the magic to be passed on.

She knew her mum had been a faerie – her dad had told her so. She'd become ill and died when Laney was really young. Would she have understood why Laney was hunting so hard for the Myricals – how she'd seen the damage caused when one Myrical fell into the hands of the Shadow and felt she had to stop it happening again?

On a sudden instinct, Laney reached up for a blue shoebox that sat on the top shelf of the bookcase. She brought it down and opened it. Her birth certificate lay on the top of a pile of papers. *15th July* – it was there in big red letters. That settled it. She had checked – there were no red moons anywhere near that date. She smiled – she was in the clear.

Under the date of birth on the certificate were two lines labelled *name of mother* and *name of father*. She gazed at her mother's name: *Cordelia*. The surname was too smudged to read, but she knew that it was *Brightsea*. It was a beautiful name that sounded like a rolling wave, especially if you said it aloud: *Cordelia Brightsea*.

She rifled underneath, picking out an envelope with some photos inside. There weren't many photos of her mum or herself when she was little. Her dad had said that some of them got lost when they packed up to move to Skellmore. She looked through them, pausing over one of her mum holding her as a little baby – a tiny, blue-eyed thing with hair like fluff. Her mum was smiling and her short brown hair was ruffled by the wind. Behind them, a mass of bare tree branches pointed up at a wintry-looking sky.

The garden in the picture seemed so familiar – probably because she'd looked at the photo so many times. She wished she could remember more about her mum. Not the big stuff, but little things like her mum's favourite food or how she'd brushed her hair. She didn't know those kinds of things because she'd only been two when her mum died.

She closed the shoebox and put it away. It was like putting away a piece of herself, but she had to go. There were Myricals to find – and first she needed to go and apologise to Gwen.

CHAPTER
7

Laney walked swiftly down the front path. The church steeple rose up on her right, grey in the morning sunshine. Laney wondered how many faerie flights that spire had seen – how many secrets it held. She turned into Beacon Way and walked down the hill. A sleek grey cat sat at the entrance to The Cattery, Claudia's crescent-shaped road, and it fixed unblinking eyes on her as she went past. Laney stared back. Sometimes she wondered if the cats knew more than she did. The Greytail house on the corner gave a long, low growl as she walked on.

Hearing shouts in the park, Laney looked through the hedge. Craig Mottle and Jack Turney were mucking around on the roundabout. A bus rumbled down the High Street and in the swirl of dust it left behind Laney caught sight of Mr Stingwood. She stopped, not wanting to run into him after what her dad had told her the day before. Stingwood was the Thorn Elder from Gillforth village who'd performed the Seeing Thread test on her when she first Awakened. He was deeply suspicious of her and she knew he'd do all he could to stop her, Fletcher and Claudia being friends.

She watched him walk up to the door of the minimart, leaning on his walking stick, and then turn sideways to fit his massive shoulders through the doorway. Just as he was halfway through, Sara Thornbeam, Fletcher's little sister, came racing round the corner, nearly bumping into him.

"Get out of it, you little—" He waved his walking stick at Sara, who ran away. His eyes were fierce underneath his bushy eyebrows.

Laney hung back until he'd disappeared inside. She would never forget the nasty spells that had come from the end of his walking stick on the night of the flood. Hurrying past the shop, she took the turning into Gnarlwood Lane. The air here usually felt quieter but more alive somehow, as if just breathing it in would make you grow. But today it didn't feel the same and the trees that lined the road creaked restlessly.

Laney knocked on Gwen's ivy-covered front door and waited. The door swung open slowly as if the wind had moved it, then Gwen stepped out of nowhere. She held a deep-purple flower in the middle of her palm and the petals clenched then opened in a steady rhythm. Laney coughed as a bittersweet smell filled her nose and throat.

"Gwen, I've come to apologise about what happened after you went out last night." Trying not to stare at the pulsing flower, Laney met Gwen's eyes and was shocked by the coldness in them.

"Do you think an apology will make up for what you've done?" Gwen said quietly, the breeze ruffling her white hair. "You destroyed my Spirit Smoke – a blend made by my mother that I have been using for nearly seventy years, and there's damage to my rowan tree that will take many months to repair."

Laney turned scarlet. "I'm so sorry! It was my fault, not Fletcher's or Claudia's. I had the idea of finding out more about the Myricals using the Spirit Smoke and—"

"The Spirit Smoke was not a toy." Gwen's voice stung like nettles. "It was made from grains of memory and experience going back hundreds of years, and held the knowledge of many generations."

"I know I shouldn't have—"

"And the rowan tree was providing ingredients for an important enchantment."

"I'm really sorry," Laney said again. "Maybe I could go and gather something from another rowan tree – that way you could still get the things you need."

"No, thank you." Gwen was silent for a moment and ivy from the walls crept over Laney's arms and down her back. "Now you will have to excuse me." And she shut the door.

Laney pulled the ivy off her clothes and retreated down the front path. She looked back at the house as she closed the garden gate. Black smoke was rising from one of the huge trumpet-shaped flowers that formed the roof. Laney turned away. She'd never seen the Thorn Elder so cross before.

When she finally crossed the river and reached the fields on the other side, she found Fletcher sitting on a fence glancing at his watch.

He jumped down when he saw her. "What did Gwen say?"

"She's really angry with me," said Laney. "You were right – we never should have used the Spirit Smoke. It was a bad idea."

"I did mend most of her plants, but there were a couple I couldn't fix," said Fletcher.

"One of the broken ones is a rowan tree that she really needed for an enchantment. She was making magic when I got there, with this purple flower that kept opening and closing its petals. Do you know what it was?"

"I'm not exactly an expert on Mystic spells." Fletcher handed Laney the adder stone and unfolded his map. "Let's start. There's no point waiting for Claudia. I bet she's still asleep."

They scanned two fields in quick succession.

"We're getting faster at this now," said Fletcher, marking them off on the map. "What's with you today? You're really quiet. Are you still worrying about what Gwen said?"

Laney checked the last field again with the adder stone. She'd actually been thinking about Mist training and the disaster of the boiling lake. "It's not that. I'm just tired of looking through the stone."

"OK, let's swap over." Fletcher took the adder stone and gave her the map.

Laney raised an eyebrow. "You're actually trusting me with the map? You've been holding on to it for six weeks. Are you sure I won't ruin it?" As she opened it out, a light rain began to fall on the paper and she hurriedly closed it up again.

"Hey, look what you did."

"What?" Laney struggled with the map that had folded up crooked.

"Look!"

Laney looked. Rain carried on falling on her head, on the grass and on Fletcher. But just above the map, a patch of raindrops hung still in the air. She reached out a finger to touch one and they all fell together. Then the rain shower stopped, leaving the grass sparkling with water.

"You held those raindrops still without realising you were doing it," said Fletcher. "I haven't seen you use your Mist powers for weeks. The training yesterday must've really helped."

"I—" began Laney.

"That's a joke," a snide voice spoke behind them. "Seeing Laney control her power is about as likely as seeing a pig win a gymnastics competition." Jessie stood there, smirking.

"So it was you making it rain," said Fletcher.

"Oh, well done. Give the stupid Thorn a medal." Jessie folded her arms. "Didn't you notice it was only raining over you and not the whole field?"

"Do you have to be like that?" Fletcher looked at Jessie steadily. "Laney actually did control her powers just then."

The wind whipped up Jessie's dark curly hair. "No, she didn't. She did it by accident again. She's always doing things *by accident*."

"I am here, you know," said Laney.

"I was trying to forget," Jessie snapped back. "What are you doing anyway? If Frogley finds out that you're spending all your time with other tribes you'll be for it."

"Yeah, and you'd love to be the one to tell him, wouldn't you?" Laney folded her arms.

"I bet your mum wouldn't be too impressed about you spending time with Laney either," Jessie told Fletcher. Suddenly she leaned towards him, trying to get a closer look at the adder stone. "What's that?"

Fletcher shoved it in his pocket. "You should go," he said shortly.

Jessie's gold-ringed eyes narrowed. "I wasn't staying anyway! But before I go, I'll show you a real Mist spell that's better than any pathetic effort from *her*." She sneered at Laney and then with a sweep of her hand she conjured an arc of water that rose out of the river and curved over the fence.

Glistening beautifully, the water lunged at Fletcher, hitting him hard and knocking him off his feet. Soaking wet, he flicked his fingers to summon a spiky bramble out of the hedge but Jessie just laughed at this move. "You won't get me with that thing. Let's face it – you Thorns aren't really winning types."

"What's your problem?" Laney moved in between them, blocking Jessie. "The only reason he hasn't beaten you already is because he's nicer than you are."

"How sweet! But that's just a sign of weakness." Jessie closed her eyes for a second and whispered something. Then she pushed Laney aside and pointed at Fletcher.

The water all over him froze instantly into a sheet of ice encasing every patch of his skin and clothes.

"No! Change him back!" Laney stared at the frozen Fletcher in horror.

"No way." Jessie's voice lowered. "I'm on to you. You can try and pretend that you're just a dopey girl who can barely lift a water drop. But I've seen stuff and I knew you were a freak ages ago. When all the other Mists see you for what you are you won't be coming back to training."

"Get lost, Jessie." Claudia vaulted neatly over the fence. "Isn't it bad enough that we'll have to see you at school on Monday?"

"Oh great!" sighed Jessie. "It's the Greytail."

Laney held Jessie's gaze and her hands glowed with heat. "Get lost, Jessie, before we make you."

"Like I said, I wasn't staying anyway." Jessie walked off without looking at Fletcher's icy figure.

Laney knelt down next to Fletcher. She could see his eyelashes, each one enclosed in frosted whiteness. Her face darkened. She would get Jessie back for this.

"Well, I suppose we have to defrost him," said Claudia. "Although I quite like him like this. Not so bossy."

"Is he all right under there?" said Laney. "He looks almost. . ." She didn't want to say dead.

"I have no idea. Ice is your department, not mine." Claudia poked one of Fletcher's ears. "Frozen solid! Weird! I wonder if he can feel anything."

"Claudia!" A sick feeling rose in Laney's chest. "I've never done any magic with ice. I've never frozen anything."

Claudia sighed. "Seriously, think about it. You don't have to *make* the ice. You just have to melt it."

Laney's brain cleared. Claudia was right. "OK, be quiet a minute." She took Fletcher's ice hands in hers and closed her eyes. *Melt . . . just melt. . .* She tried to imagine the ice turning to water and dripping off his fingers.

"Er . . . I think you should stop now," said Claudia.

Laney opened her eyes to find steam gently rising from Fletcher's clothes and his hair standing on end. He blinked, dazed. "Wow, I feel really warm. What happened? Where did Jessie go?"

"She scarpered after turning you into an ice cube," said Claudia. "Laney's just thawed you out."

"Urgh!" Fletcher wrung water out of his sleeve. "That's why everything went white. At least she didn't get a proper look at the adder stone. I really don't want her finding out what we're doing."

"I don't think she knows anything," said Laney.

Claudia turned to her. "Good job, Water Girl. I don't know why you're worrying so much – you'll make a great member of the Mist tribe."

Laney wished she felt so sure. Jessie's words echoed inside her head: *I've seen stuff and I knew you were a freak ages ago.*

What had she meant? Laney's powers had only emerged six weeks ago. Before that, she had just been a human with no powers at all. There had been nothing to see.

CHAPTER 8

After two more days of Myrical hunting even Fletcher had to admit they weren't getting much further. Claudia wanted to hatch an elaborate plan to pay Jessie back but Fletcher refused to be a part of it.

"She isn't powerful enough to make permanent ice," he said. "That thin stuff she used didn't hurt me. Just leave it."

"If we try to get revenge, Jessie might come after us again," added Laney. "She's already starting to wonder why we're hanging out together."

Jessie wasn't the only one who wondered. When Laney climbed reluctantly on to the school bus on that first Monday morning, there was a sudden break in the conversations around her. Feeling as if everyone was watching her, she made her way down the bus. The kids were divided up just as they'd always been. The faeries sat bunched together in their tribes away from the humans. Laney's heart missed a beat knowing that most people couldn't see which faces had gold-ringed eyes. Last term, before Awakening, she'd never known why everyone split into gangs like this.

Fletcher was with the older Thorns at the back. Claudia was sitting with some Greytail girls from Pyton. They all had a similar stylish look with streaked hair and earrings, and they were leaning towards each other, laughing. Laney headed towards them but Claudia warned her off with a tiny shake of the head. So she turned back, finding a place near the front by the window. She couldn't sit with the Mists her own age – Jessie was there.

When they got to school she went in search of Steph. The corridors were heaving with kids and the occasional shout of a teacher rang out above the general buzz, telling them to hurry to their form rooms.

"Hey, Dreamy!" Steph tapped her on the shoulder. "I've been calling you for ages. Did you have a good summer? Shame you couldn't come into town more."

"I know – my dad was too busy to give me a lift most of the time." Laney pushed away a twinge of guilt about lying to her friend. The real reason was that the search for the Myricals had taken up all her time but she was bound by her promise to keep the faerie world a secret.

"What's up?" Steph studied Laney's face. "Are you worried that everyone will talk about you breaking the water fountain on the last day of term? I think they've all forgotten."

"Someone's bound to go on about it." Laney glanced at Craig Mottle, who was yelling across the corridor. "There are some things you just can't get away from."

After registration they made their way to the science lab and Laney scanned the faces around her, counting the pairs of gold-ringed eyes in the crowd. A strange feeling settled around her heart. Her old life had been about school and friends and she'd always thought of the faerie world as separate from that. It was stupid really – she should have known she couldn't just go back to ordinary life at school and only be a Mist when she was in Skellmore. She got out her book and her pens and tried to look normal but the pens rolled off the desk on to the floor.

"Are you sure you're all right?" said Steph. "You're acting all twitchy. Has something happened you haven't told me about?"

"I'm fine – just tired." Laney bent down to pick up the pens.

"Right, we're doing an experiment on materials that conduct electricity," Dr Direley, their science teacher, called over the noise. "I need some help . . . let's see. Laney. Fill a dozen beakers with water and bring them to the front, please. Water is one of the materials we'll be testing. Jessie, please bring that box of leads."

The room went silent. Laney went to the sink and turned on the tap. She felt the pressure of all the gold-ringed eyes that she knew would be looking at her. She could guess what they were thinking – that she would do something weird to the water: make it boil or turn a different colour. They thought she wouldn't be able to control herself and keep her Mist power hidden.

"You can't let Laney do it, sir. She'll break everything," said Craig Mottle. "She's the one that bust the water fountain on the last day of term."

"If you want to discuss it, Craig, you can come and see me at the end of school," Dr Direley replied.

Hands shaking a little, Laney arranged the beakers in a row and began filling them. From the corner of her eye she could see Steph looking round in a puzzled way as she noticed the tension in the room. She stood the beakers on a tray and took them to the teacher. The water in every one was still and clear. She couldn't resist a triumphant glance at Jessie, but the other girl wasn't even looking.

"Now, before you begin let's remind ourselves of some facts about electricity." Dr Direley drifted into a monotone. "Here's a picture of a lightning strike taken in Mexico. Lightning occurs when a cloud fills up with electrical charges." He clicked his remote and a picture of red forked lightning appeared on the screen.

Laney couldn't breathe. This was the Shadow's attack spell – the red lightning – and it seemed ready to leap out of the screen at her. She jerked backwards, knocking one of the beakers with her hand. It tipped over and rolled off the worktop, smashing on to the floor.

"I told you, sir," said Craig.

"I'm sorry." Laney hid her trembling hands behind her back. "I'll get something to sweep it up."

Everyone sat in the same groups on the bus journey home at the end of the day. Resigned to it, Laney sat by herself and watched the fields roll past the window. She glanced up as an older boy moved to the seat behind hers.

"Mist training's at eight o'clock tomorrow night," he muttered. "Don't use your wings to get there – don't forget."

Laney gave a slight nod, her insides lurching. Another chance to join Mist training – that had to be a good thing, didn't it?

When the bus got to Skellmore, she waited outside the minimart for Fletcher and Claudia. Cathy Rainer and Leah Millbrook, the girls from Mist training, stared at her as they passed. Leah straightened her glasses and whispered something to her friend, and Laney's heart sank.

Fletcher came over. "We need to carry on our search tonight," he said quietly. "Let's meet in the field behind the yard at seven."

"See you then," said Laney, and Fletcher crossed the High Street heading for Gnarlwood Lane and home.

"It's always work, work, work," Claudia grumbled. "When can we have some time off?"

"I bet the Shadow hasn't stopped looking, wherever he is, so we can't either." Laney shivered. She knew she shouldn't talk of the Shadow, but she couldn't help it. It felt like they were always waiting, wondering when he'd appear again. It was starting to get on her nerves.

"You seriously need to chill out about the Shadow," Claudia told her as they walked up Beacon Way. "He hasn't been seen for weeks. Maybe he's gone for good."

"I doubt it. Sometimes I really get the feeling he's not far away." Laney didn't add that she even thought she'd seen him a couple of times but it had turned out to be nothing.

"If he was, I reckon I'd know first – Greytail senses are basically perfect. Catch you later." Claudia turned into The Cattery.

Laney carried on up the hill. She didn't understand how Claudia had put their encounter with the Shadow on the night of the flood out of her mind so easily. It must be nice to live in the now without worrying about the past or future. Maybe it was time to admit to the others that she was still freaked out about the Shadow. She had faced him, fought him and yet now she felt more terrified than before. Knowing exactly how someone became a Shadow made it worse. She could imagine how, after a faerie died, someone had gathered the only thing that remained: the dust. Then they'd used it to create a powerful dark spell. She suddenly wondered whose body the Shadow faerie had used that very first time and the thought made her stomach turn over.

She stepped sideways to avoid a small cloud of sprites hovering over the pavement. Now she had to think of a good excuse to tell Kim why she needed to go out on a school night. Luckily, Kim was in a good mood and happily accepted Laney's excuse about preparing for a geography field trip. This was partly true, as they'd been given a letter about a trip to study the environment in a few weeks' time. Just as she was explaining about the homework, Simon, her dad's workmate, called in to grab some work tools from the garage and Kim forgot to ask any more.

Laney got to the yard behind the minimart at seven o'clock and found Claudia sitting on the fence. "Where's Fletcher?" she asked, surprised.

Claudia jerked her head at a maple tree in the field behind them. "He's camouflaged up there. I saw him straight away but I couldn't be bothered to tell him that. You can't fool a Greytail."

Laney climbed the fence and walked round the

tree, trying to spot him. "Fletcher, what are you doing?"

As soon as he moved she could see him, halfway up, slouching against the tree trunk. He grinned and jumped down.

"Don't want to be seen with us then?" said Laney.

"Just practising for the next Thorn training. It's better if we're not seen together too much anyway."

"Thorn training probably means talking to flowers and singing to trees," Claudia whispered to Laney.

"You talk to cats, so what's the difference?" said Laney.

Fletcher got out his map. "I think we should start checking Hobbin Forest today. We've put it off for ages because it's such a big place to search. Now it's time to go in."

Claudia switched from funny to fierce in an instant. "Just because you're a Thorn doesn't mean we have to search the forest first."

"Don't worry," Fletcher said calmly. "I can read the trees for signs of danger. You'll be safe in there with me."

Claudia's eyes narrowed. "Last time I looked I could take care of myself."

Laney grabbed the map. The roughly drawn lines of the river and the roads curved across the paper. Most of the fields and farmland around Skellmore were already ticked off. Checking the village itself would be far too tricky during daylight.

"What happened to searching each place in order?" Claudia said. "I bet the forest isn't the next place on that map."

Laney looked from Fletcher's serious face to the mass of trees on the other side of the field. There had always been something odd about Hobbin Forest. It didn't seem like an evil place, just very old, as if it knew ancient secrets it would never share. People would come and go while the forest remained, wrapped in its own mystery and not caring about the wave of human life sweeping by. Wouldn't the Shadow find it the perfect place to hide?

She lifted her chin. Maybe going in there and facing her fear would get rid of it. "We have to check the forest sometime," she said. "I think we should just get it over with."

"Fine," said Claudia. "But it's a huge place. It's going to take ages."

They hurried towards the forest. Laney tried to keep up with Claudia's long graceful strides. She looked up at the dark treeline just before they plunged inside. A mob of crows flew squawking above the topmost branches, filling the air with their ragged black wings.

CHAPTER
9

Fletcher led them deep into the forest, stopping now and then to check the lines on a tree trunk. Each time the crows broke into their rough chorus, Claudia paused, looking into the treetops and listening intently. As they walked on, the channels of sunlight coming through the branches began to fade.

"Right. If we start from this log, we can check a small area at a time and then come back here before we search the other way." Fletcher pointed to a huge fallen tree covered with moss and fungi. In the half-light it looked like a resting giant.

"Searching here will be harder than it was in the fields," said Laney. "We need to circle round every tree and bramble patch so we don't miss anything."

"We can mark the trees so we know where we've checked," said Claudia.

"No, we can't!" Fletcher said sharply. "Not unless you want the whole Thorn tribe on your case."

"All right!" Claudia rolled her eyes. "Chill! It was just an idea."

"I'll start." Laney took the adder stone from Fletcher. "We'll have to stop once it's dark. I know we can see in the dark better than a human, but we don't know how clear the signs will be. We could miss something."

"Actually, I took this from my dad's shed." Fletcher drew what looked like a white china globe out of his pocket. "I figured I could put it back before he realises it's missing."

"Sweet." Claudia nodded. "Can you light it though?"

Fletcher shook the orb and a pale glow flickered inside it. "It's got a little bit of power left. That'll have to do." He released the orb into the air, where it floated just over their heads.

Laney put the adder stone to her eye and began scanning the forest carefully for the telltale shimmer of spell vibrations. The orb followed her and so did Fletcher, marking things off on the map.

Suddenly he put his ear to a tree trunk. "I don't get it. Today there's nothing. It's like the trees don't want to talk."

"It isn't just the trees that are acting weird." Claudia jumped down from a high branch where she'd been sitting. "The crows were making warning calls when we ran into the wood and now they've gone completely silent."

"They were making warning calls?" Laney shivered. "Why didn't you tell us before?"

Claudia raised her eyebrows. "You were the one who was all *we have to check the forest sometime.* She put on a mimicking voice. *"We should get it over with."* A tree branch behind her whipped against her legs and she leapt away. "Hey! Stop it!" She glared at Fletcher.

"I didn't make it move, I swear," he said.

There was a scraping above their heads and another long branch shifted downwards to point at them like an accusing finger.

"OK, this is freaking me out now." Laney looked at Fletcher and his worried expression made her even more nervous. "Why are they—" A rustling noise began near her foot. Heart jumping, she grabbed the orb from the air and shone it on the ground. At first all she could see was earth. Then she caught a small movement among the fallen leaves. A knotted brown thing was creeping along, slowly pushing twigs and leaves aside.

"What is it?" said Claudia with a shudder. "It's disgusting!"

Two more knotted brown things crept over the ground like ancient crooked fingers. Laney took a sharp breath. She recognised their twisted shape. "They're tree roots. I saw one move like that on my way to Mist training three nights ago. I told you, remember?"

"You're right – they are tree roots," said Fletcher. "But what are they doing out of the ground? Only really high-level Thorns can do something like this and I'm sure there's no one else around. Pass me the adder stone a sec." He held out his hand for the stone.

Laney threw it to him and he looked at the roots

through the hole. "There's no sign of a spell," he said at last. "At least, nothing I can see with the stone."

One of the roots climbed on to Laney's trainer and as she kicked it off she heard a faint, far-off scream.

Claudia's eyebrows shot up wildly. "That's a human!"

"Are you sure?" Laney said quickly.

"Yes. Come on!" Claudia flew up through the tangled branches.

Leaving the orb behind, they soared into the night sky. Air streamed past Laney's wings and the forest blurred beneath her, turned silver by the half-moon.

The cry sounded again. It was closer now.

Claudia hovered above a tall beech tree and Laney knew she must be using her Greytail tracking skills. Suddenly she pointed down through the branches. "There!" she said. "Right below us."

Laney plunged downwards, leaves and branches scraping against her wings. She landed and changed back to human form instantly. It was dark without the orb and her eyes took a moment to get used to the blackness. Claudia landed behind her, then Fletcher.

"Help!" yelled a boy. "Help, somebody!"

"That sounds like Craig Mottle," said Laney.

Claudia sniffed the air delicately. "Yep,

that's Craig."

"I didn't know you could tell people apart by smell," muttered Laney.

"I can't always," said Claudia. "But Craig is truly unmistakable."

Fletcher pushed through the trees in the direction of the shouting. "Hi, is that you, Craig?" he called. "Can you stop shining that thing in my eyes?"

Laney followed the waving beam of torchlight through a gap in the trees. Fletcher crossed the clearing in a few strides and knelt down next to Craig.

"I'm stuck, man." Craig's voice shook. "I can't move."

"Give me the torch," said Claudia, and the torchlight stopped swaying.

Craig lay flat on his back with long knobbly roots wound round his arms and ankles. He was bound tight to the earth, only able to move his head. Laney gaped at the tree roots. There were so many of them.

"How did this happen?" cried Fletcher.

"I don't know! Just help me, man." Craig struggled. "I can't get these things off me."

Fletcher took hold of the root that was curled round Craig's ankle and yanked on it. His face grew red as the stem pulled away but as soon as he let go it snapped back into place.

Craig groaned. "These things are tight. I can't feel my right foot any more. I don't understand how they got so twisted."

Laney, Claudia and Fletcher retreated to the other side of the clearing. "Those roots – it's like they worked together to tie him up," whispered Laney. "How can they do that? Roots can't think!"

"Someone could think for them," said Fletcher.

Claudia shone the torch back at Craig lying immobile on the ground. "The way the trees are acting tonight, I could believe anything."

Fletcher looked through the adder stone. "I can't see any spell shimmer and why would anyone want to capture Craig anyway?"

They exchanged looks and Laney said what they were all thinking. "Maybe the Shadow doesn't need a reason. And maybe there's no spell shimmer because his dark magic doesn't leave that kind of trace."

"But if the Shadow had been here, we'd see withered leaves and dead branches – remember how he turned the plants brown before, as if he sucked the life out of things?" said Claudia.

Laney gripped her hands to stop them shaking. Suddenly the wood seemed thicker and every pocket of darkness was filled with something that lurked. "What about hobgobbits?" she suggested, thinking of the fierce creatures that lived in the forest. "They don't exactly like people walking through their parts of the wood."

"No, they wouldn't have left him like this," said Fletcher.

"Let's untie him and get out of here," said Claudia.

"We can't let Craig see our powers and I don't know how we're going to free him without using them," said Fletcher.

"There's a trance spell I'm learning at Greytail training." Claudia's eyes gleamed. "I'm not great at it, but if I manage it it would knock him out nicely. After the human comes out of the trance they forget what happened just before the spell."

"It's too risky," said Fletcher.

"It's all we've got," said Laney sharply. "Do it! We need to get out of here."

CHAPTER
10

"What are you guys doing? Stop talking and help me – there's something crawling over my neck!" yelped Craig.

Laney rushed back across the clearing. A long gnarled root had coiled itself round Craig's throat. He struggled, his face pale in the torchlight.

"Stop moving. You're making it pull tighter." As Fletcher spoke, the earth underneath Craig's leg cracked open and another root emerged, curling round his knee.

Claudia let out a faint hiss. "I swear it's trying to pull him into the ground."

"What! What do you mean? They're just brambles, aren't they?" Craig's voice rose in panic and the crack in the earth opened wider.

Fletcher grabbed the nearest root and shot a warning look at Claudia. "Calm down, Craig. We're not going to let anything happen to you. Just try to lie still."

Laney's heart thudded erratically. This had to be the Shadow's work – it was like he was showing off his strength. "Do that thing you talked about, Claudia!" she said. "We need to make this quick."

"OK." Claudia handed Laney the torch and knelt down next to Craig, her face frozen in concentration.

"What's going on?" Craig moaned. "Stop staring at me."

"Be quiet if you want us to free your useless lump

of bones!" snapped Claudia. Then with an effort she softened her voice. "Now . . . relax and look at me."

Laney tried to hold the torch steady. What if the Shadow was close by? She tried to concentrate on Claudia, who was performing a complicated series of blinks, as if she was sending a message with her eyes. Craig began blinking too and at last his eyes turned glassy even though they remained wide open.

Claudia waved a hand in front of his face but he didn't react. She sprang up. "It's done, but it won't last long. Your turn now, Thorn Boy."

Fletcher started trying to untangle the root coiled round Craig's neck. The wind moved the branches overhead. From the corner of her eye, Laney thought she could see a dark shape near the top of one tree. It hung from a branch, moving as the tree swayed. Her skin prickled and she pointed the torch upwards to find it was only leaves. A shiver passed across her skin again. She couldn't do this any more – getting shivers at every patch of darkness, jumping at every noise. She had to do something. Throwing down the torch, she held her hands above the ground. She would use Mist power – produce water from the earth to blast the roots away. She closed her eyes and focused. *Water come out – break the roots. . .*

"Laney, what are you doing?" said Fletcher.

She opened her eyes, her concentration broken. "Just trying something with Mist power." She took hold of a root and scrunched up her face as she tried to focus again. Her hands grew hot and the root darkened from brown to black. Then it pinged loose and uncoiled from Craig's arm before slithering away across the ground.

Fletcher's mouth dropped open. "What?"

Laney seized the root round Craig's neck. That blackened too before unravelling completely.

Claudia stared. "Who knew Mist power would work on roots! Keep going; get rid of all of them before he wakes up."

Laney grasped each root one by one. Some of them tried to cling on to Craig but once she tightened her hold they gave in. Craig stirred and gave a moan, but his eyes stayed glassy. At last all the roots had released their hold on him.

"He's still in the trance," said Claudia. "Let's go now and when he wakes up he won't remember we were here."

"We should stay close enough to make sure the roots don't get hold of him again," said Laney. "I know he's annoying but—" She broke off as a root looped around her ankle and pulled tight. A second root coiled around the other ankle, digging in viciously. She lost her balance, falling flat on the ground.

"Stay still!" Fletcher crouched down. "I'll try and grab them."

"Yeah – well, I can't move much anyway!" Laney managed to reach the tough roots entangling her legs and pull them off. They wriggled in her hand and, disgusted, she threw them across the clearing where they slithered over the earth like huge worms before burying themselves into the ground next to a tree trunk.

"Fly, Laney!" Claudia changed to faerie form and soared upwards.

Laney transformed too and hovered in the air, but Fletcher stayed in human form, staring around in bewilderment.

Claudia pulled Laney behind a tree. "Craig's coming out of the trance," she whispered.

"Hey!" Craig staggered up. "What's going on?"

"You were asleep," said Fletcher. "I just found you here."

"My legs feel really weird. Pins and needles, I guess." Craig yawned and picked up the torch. "What are you doing here anyway?"

"Er, I just came for a walk," muttered Fletcher.

"Uh, I should go." Craig stumbled away through the trees and eventually the sound of snapping twigs grew fainter.

Laney and Claudia flew down after they were sure Craig had gone. Laney kept a wary eye on the ground but the roots didn't reappear. Fletcher rubbed his hands on his jeans. "I just don't get it. Tree roots don't do that by themselves."

"We should go and collect the orb. Then we have to tell Gwen about this," said Claudia.

Laney remembered the coldness in Gwen's eyes when she'd gone to apologise for ruining the Spirit Smoke. "Do you think it's a good idea to bother her? She was pretty busy when I saw her a few days ago."

"We have to – this is important." Fletcher took out the adder stone and scanned the clearing again. He circled every tree and even changed to faerie form and flew up to check the canopy. "There's still no sign of any spell shimmer," he told the others.

"Let me see." Laney took the adder stone and scanned the clearing. "No, there's nothing."

"Shhh!" hissed Claudia. "Someone's coming."

The wind rose for a moment, sending the topmost branches swaying. Laney put the adder stone in her pocket and crouched down, the skin prickling on her arms. Away to the left, a tall man with massive shoulders came striding through the trees, swinging a walking stick. Even in the dark, Laney recognised his fierce eyes and heavy eyebrows. "Stingwood," she whispered.

The trees swept their branches to one side to let him pass. As he came to the edge of the clearing, the ground trembled as if the tree roots were moving once more. He stopped and stared at the place where Craig had lain, trapped. His gold-ringed eyes shone bright in the gloom. Then he marched deeper into the trees.

Laney, Claudia and Fletcher stayed hidden for a while after he'd gone. Shivers ran up and down Laney's arms. Stingwood had a cruel side and he was the Elder she was most afraid of, even though he was a Thorn like Gwen.

"I think he's gone," muttered Claudia at last.

"Did you see how he stared at the place where Craig got trapped?" said Laney. "It was like he expected Craig still to be there. Do you think he's the one that made the roots go wild?"

"Maybe," said Fletcher. "But I've never seen anything like that root spell before."

Together they flew up through the branches and Laney took a deep breath of night air, happy to be free of the forest. After collecting the orb, they flew straight back to Skellmore, passing over Craig who was limping across a field. On the outskirts, they changed to human form before running over to Gnarlwood Lane. A small figure stood on the path in front of Gwen's garden gate.

"What are you doing up?" Fletcher stared at his little sister. "It's way past your bedtime."

"Password?" said Sara Thornbeam.

"We're in a hurry. Get out the way," said Claudia.

"Nope." Sara folded her little arms. "Password?"

"Sara, stop it!" said Fletcher. "Shouldn't you be in bed?"

"Mum sent me out to play," said Sara. "Gwen's not at home anyway. She went out."

"Where did she go?" Fletcher demanded.

"Don't know. Gathering stuff, I think – she took her basket," said Sara.

Fletcher's forehead creased. "If Mum sent you out at this time of night, something's going on." He strode down the lane to his house, which had branches covering the walls edged with red and white berries.

Laney shrugged at Claudia and they both followed. Sara crept along behind them. Through the window, they saw the inside of the Thornbeam house which was lit with a warm glow. In the kitchen, a dozen people sat at the large table; more stood round the walls. Empty mugs and plates were everywhere.

Fletcher's dad, Mr Thornbeam, sat at the head of the table. Laney always thought he had a kind face but today his weather-worn features were drawn into a deep frown. Laney leaned closer to listen.

"He is changing things much too fast." Mr Thornbeam looked thoughtfully at the Thorns around him. "He's not taking time to think about what he's doing."

"Who are they talking about?" Claudia whispered.

Fletcher shrugged and pulled Sara out of sight of the window.

"We all need to consider what this project will mean," added Mr Thornbeam.

"These are fine words, Glen! But too often we've been slow to act," snapped a man with ginger hair. "And because of that the other tribes don't respect us."

Mr Thornbeam said quietly, "I don't care what the other tribes think. I care about the future of *our* tribe. The truth is that those who say they are seeking to make us more powerful could bring us all down."

The ginger-haired man thumped his fist on the table. "Every year it gets worse – the chemicals they put on the land, the tree clearing. . . These are things we can hardly ignore!"

The noise inside grew as several people spoke at once. Then they all started to get up and after a moment the front door opened. Fletcher beckoned Laney and Claudia round the corner and they hid behind the bushy wall. A stream of Thorns came out of the front door and plodded away down the lane. Mr Thornbeam stood watching them for a while, his eyebrows lowered reflectively. Then he went back inside.

"Did they leave any cake?" Sara dashed inside to search for leftovers.

"What was that all about?" Claudia asked Fletcher. "The Thorns must know that something's going on in the woods. Why else would they be so serious?"

"I'll talk to my dad and see if I can find out anything," said Fletcher.

"I want to know what Stingwood was doing in the forest," said Laney. "I don't trust him. I think we should follow him."

"Don't, Laney." Fletcher frowned. "Just leave it."

"We have to work out what he's up to," Laney insisted. "Listen – Shadow faeries must have a human form like we do, right?"

Claudia shivered and glanced round. Fletcher's face went very still.

Laney tried to swallow. It felt like the words were stuck in her throat. "What if we *have* seen the Shadow and we just didn't know it?" she continued. "What if the Shadow is Stingwood?"

CHAPTER 11

"Don't you think we'd have noticed something different about Stingwood if he really was the Shadow?" said Claudia. "Seriously! No one can pretend to be normal all the time, can they? He'd have given himself away by now."

"I think the Shadow lives right here in Skellmore." Laney stifled a shiver. "Sometimes I think I can feel he's around here somewhere. He knows that we found one Myrical and I bet he knows we're searching for more. He could have been watching us for weeks."

"I don't know." Fletcher rubbed his hair. "Maybe you're letting your imagination take over. I've been looking out for signs of Shadow magic – like withered plants, dying trees – and I haven't seen anything."

"He'll be covering up where he's been and what he's doing, won't he?" said Laney. "If it *is* Stingwood, we need to follow him and see what he's up to!"

"No!" said Fletcher firmly. "Shadow magic is extremely powerful. If Stingwood *is* the Shadow he probably has ways of knowing whether someone's watching him." Fletcher looked hard at Laney. "I'll find out from my dad what the other Thorns know and then we can work out what to do next. In the meantime, promise you won't do anything stupid."

"I wasn't going to do anything stupid," said

Laney, a little annoyed. "I just want to keep an eye on Stingwood."

"It's not just that," Fletcher said seriously. "It's about you as well. That thing you did to the roots . . . I don't understand how you did it! You're not a Thorn. You shouldn't have power over things that grow like we do."

"This is about the Wolf Moon, isn't it?" Laney's stomach turned over painfully.

"No, I'm saying that you've only just Awakened and you said your first training session didn't go very well. Maybe you need to work on controlling what you're doing. So it's not so . . . random."

"So my powers aren't good enough now? Is that what you mean?" hissed Laney.

"Don't stress out," Fletcher said with infuriating calmness. "I'm just saying that what you did to the roots was strange, that's all."

"If it's freaking you out, then I'd rather search for the Myricals on my own!" said Laney.

The front door opened. "Who's out there?" called Mr Thornbeam.

"It's me, Dad," called Fletcher, before lowering his voice to a whisper. "Look, I'm sorry, Laney! I wasn't saying we shouldn't search together. Just that you need to walk before you run."

He sounded just like Frogley at the training session. Laney's hands grew hot. She turned on her heel and hurried up the lane, a dull ache inside her. Maybe Fletcher had been thinking those things about her for weeks: that she wasn't in control, that she was a problem.

"Wait up, Water Girl!" Claudia sprinted beside her. "You can't really want to look for the Myricals on your own. It's boring enough searching for them together."

"Aren't I freaking you out, too?" snapped Laney.

"It *is* weird that you got those roots to let go of Craig so easily, but I'm not freaking out about it," said Claudia. "Maybe your Mist Elders can help you understand your powers better – they're the ones to ask."

Laney thought of Frogley and sighed. She had as much chance of getting help from him as getting Toby to fly.

They turned right into the High Street and passed the empty park. There was a light on in the minimart and a cloud of silver sprites circled a lamppost before fluttering away up the hill. Laney and Claudia walked up Beacon Way in silence. Dozens of cats perched statue-like on trees, cars and fences near the entrance to The Cattery. They turned their faces to Laney and their eyes gleamed in the darkness. A few leapt down to greet Claudia, mewing.

Laney caught her breath as a dark figure moved

quickly towards them but then she realised it was just Tom Lionhart, Claudia's older brother.

"All right, sis." Tom thrust his hands into his pockets. "You'd better get inside. You're too young to be running around this late."

"Who put you in charge?" said Claudia. "We've been rescuing Craig Mottle from rampaging tree roots without needing *your* help."

"You what?" Tom's eyes narrowed. "Where did you find him?"

"In a clearing on the north side of Hobbin Forest." Claudia waved her hand and the crowd of cats around her dispersed.

"Don't go down there," said Laney. "It's not safe."

But Tom wasn't listening. "I knew it'd all start up again as soon as everything was quiet," he muttered. "You two had better stay out of the forest from now on. The Thorns have been making trouble in there for weeks. They want to be the ruling tribe. They always have!" He whistled to a sleek grey cat, which sprang quickly after him.

A familiar figure rounded the corner and began staggering up Beacon Way. "That's Craig. At least he made it back all right, though I can't believe I'm pleased about it," said Claudia softly, and she melted away into the dark.

Not wanting to speak to Craig, Laney hurried away too. When she got home she went straight upstairs and sank on to her bed. Maybe Claudia was right and she should talk over her magic problems with someone from her own tribe. Not Frogley, he was awful. But the other one, Joe Fenworth, had been nice. She could ask her dad, but what if he stopped her from going to training once he knew what was happening?

She looked out of the window at the empty street below. It felt as if she was the only one left awake in Skellmore. Her hands still felt hot and they left faint smudge marks on the windowsill. She opened the window a bit wider, letting in more air to cool her down. A distant gleam of gold came from the massive oak tree in the park as it drew in power from the faerie ring.

She thought of Stingwood and how suspicious he'd been that she had Awakened on the night of the red moon. That could have just been a way of diverting attention from himself. He'd want to do that if he really was the Shadow. . .

Laney kept away from Craig the next day, just in case something jogged his memory about the night before. But he swaggered down the school corridor just the same as usual and for a second she wished he would remember how scared he'd been in the wood.

Fletcher caught up with her and Claudia when

they got off the bus after school. "I talked to my dad last night and I found out loads," he began.

"Flapping ears at six o'clock," said Claudia.

"Huh?" Fletcher looked confused. "Flapping what?"

Claudia sighed. "Jessie's right behind us, trying to listen to our conversation."

With a stony face, Jessie pushed past them and went into the hairdresser's where her mum worked.

"So . . . what did you find out?" Laney asked Fletcher.

Fletcher checked that no one else was near them. "Stingwood's told all the Thorns that he's setting up something in Hobbin Forest called the Avalon project. He wants to create a place that no human will be able to reach because of the enchantments surrounding it, something that will be a haven for Thorn faeries. Trouble is, no one can get in while he's setting it up, not even other faeries, which is why it's making everyone suspicious. I'm not really supposed to tell you all this – it's a Thorn secret!"

Claudia rolled her eyes. "Do the Thorns really think we'll want to join their little secret project?"

They stopped talking abruptly. The Lionhart pet shop door opened and Mrs Mottle trundled out with her dog and a bagful of doggie treats. She stared at them distrustfully before walking on and the gigantic cat's eyes on the pet shop wall swivelled in her direction as she crossed the street.

Fletcher kept his voice low. "It's all Stingwood's idea and he's channelling as much power as he can into it. My dad refused to join in. He reckons Stingwood's trying to go back to the old days before faeries and humans lived together, and he says it'll never work and Stingwood needs to face reality." He paused and then added, "So whatever Stingwood's doing to make this Avalon place must be affecting the rest of the forest and making the trees act strange."

"But he could still be the Shadow," Claudia muttered. "The whole project thing could just be a cover."

"He's definitely horrible enough to be the Shadow," said Laney. "And I still want to see what he's up to."

"Laney, don't go spying on him. It's too risky." Fletcher gave her a serious look. "Where shall we meet tonight? We'd better keep out of the forest but—"

Laney cut him off. "I've got training. So I can't come."

Fletcher pulled his bag over his shoulder. "Tomorrow then. Where shall we—"

"I can't meet then either." Laney's hands grew hot and the sore patch on her middle finger throbbed. "Like I said last night, if you don't trust my magic

I'm going to search by myself." She walked off, leaving Fletcher and Claudia staring after her.

A few minutes later she wished she hadn't said it but she was too proud to go back and find her friends again. It was obvious that Fletcher thought her powers were a problem. She was used to Jessie thinking she was rubbish but knowing that Fletcher thought so too really hurt. And the worst thing was he was right.

CHAPTER 12

Joe Fenworth didn't come to the Mist training session that evening, so Laney didn't have a chance to ask him about her powers. Standing on the shore of Faymere Lake with the other Mist kids, she just hoped she could get through the session without doing anything strange. She raised a water drop from the surface of the lake and let it fall again, breathing out in relief. Some of the Sevensies looked over and giggled, but she didn't care.

Frogley called them closer after releasing enough blue vapour to form a barrier around the lake. He folded his angular arms and his eyes swept over them, resting on Laney for a second. "Today we'll change to faerie form and use our water wings," he began.

"Yes!" The whole group grinned at each other.

Frogley droned on for a while about the skill of using water wings and how to perform various manoeuvres in the water, from back glides to plummets. Then he went on for a while about achieving "maximum efficiency" by adjusting your wings to be water-dynamic. Finally he organised everyone into small groups, each headed by one of the older kids.

Laney waited impatiently for her group's turn. Her hands felt hot but she took a deep breath and told herself to calm down. Everyone was in faerie form now and the air buzzed with the sound of beating wings.

"Next group," said Frogley.

Laney followed her group to the diving-off point.

"Wait!" Frogley ordered. He was looking at Laney over his half-moon spectacles and her heart sank. Surely he wouldn't stop her from going? He muttered a few words to their group leader, a tall boy with dark-green wings, and then waved them on.

The group leader gave them the signal to go and Laney launched into a curving dive, tucked her wings in tight and slid smoothly into the water. She'd flown in the river before, but the lake was murkier and it took a moment to get used to seeing through the water. Their group leader beckoned them on. Laney gazed around as she flew, amazed at the number of fish among the waving plant fronds.

They dived deeper and the group leader took out an orb to help light the way. The younger kids darted around, chasing and tagging each other. Laney caught sight of something below, half hidden by clouds of silt. A tall stone structure rose straight up from the bottom of the lake. If she hadn't been underwater she would have gasped but none of the rest of the group seemed surprised.

Laney flew down to get a better look and circled

the crumbling stones. This was obviously a wall but who would have built a wall down here? She saw another pile of stones and glided towards it. Diving through a hole, she found herself enclosed by stone walls on all sides. This had to be some sort of house and the hole she'd come through had to be the door. A stone roof cut out the light from above. It was quite a small and simple building.

She blinked. Standing here and looking up at the roof was oddly familiar. The pattern of the rectangular stones overhead jogged something in her mind. She had a sudden feeling that she'd been here before. It wasn't a memory exactly, but a feeling of recognition.

Realising she could lose track of her group, Laney turned back to the doorway and found three figures blocking it. Jessie hovered there with Cathy and Leah right behind her. Jessie rubbed her fingers together and they turned blue with frost. Cathy and Leah copied her. Then raising their hands, the three girls blasted jets of frost at the doorway, turning the hole to a solid block of ice.

It was done in seconds and Laney was alone.

Panicking, she flew at the doorway and bashed the ice with her fists. It didn't move. Beyond the thick, frozen wall she could see shadows moving. No doubt Jessie and her mates were having a good laugh before they flew away.

She stepped back and tried to breathe slowly. She'd melted the frost around Fletcher that time so maybe she could melt this too. She placed her palms on the ice and closed her eyes. *Warm up . . . melt. . .* she told it. She felt the ice soften but when she opened her eyes again she'd only made a small hollow in the thick surface.

She'd been angry that time when Fletcher was frozen and that had made her hands grow hotter, she was sure of it. So maybe if she could make herself feel that way again. . .

Picturing Jessie's sneering face as she'd frozen the doorway, Laney put her hands on the ice again. She felt her fingers glow with heat and in a few minutes a hole had melted in the frozen wall. As soon as it was big enough she climbed through, spread her water wings and zoomed upwards. Her group was nowhere to be seen so she broke through the lake surface and circled round to get her bearings before making her way back to the shore.

A large group was gathered at the water's edge.

"You! It had to be you." Frogley's bony jaw was tight with fury. "You abandoned your group leader and you were seen damaging the ancient Mist dwellings on the lake bottom."

"No, I didn't. . ." Laney's head whirled as she thought of the underwater houses being lived in by ancient Mist faeries. "I mean, I went to look at the buildings but I didn't damage them." She caught sight of Jessie hanging back behind Frogley, looking smug.

"This is intolerable!" Frogley puffed out his scrawny chest. "In fact, as Mist Elder I've decided that I can no longer have you at training. You are a menace to our tribe. How can the Thorns and the Greytails respect us, if we train someone like you?"

"I didn't do anything, honestly," said Laney. "I went into one of the underwater houses and some people blocked the doorway, so I broke out again – that's all. I just want to learn and improve my skills."

"You will *never* be taught all our skills and you will *never* become a full member of our tribe." Mr Frogley raised his voice, letting the words roll off his tongue. He pointed one skinny arm at the path that led away from the lake. "Go and do not return. Tomorrow I shall inform your father of my decision."

Laney's face burned. She closed her eyes, changed back to human form and made her way through the crowd of Mist kids. Jessie's face was now blank and her arms were folded. Cathy looked shocked and Leah had turned away.

Laney walked on, unblinking, until she'd gone round a corner out of sight of the lake. Then she sat down on a tree stump and put her chin in her hands. It was over. Her plan to become good at Mist spells had lasted for two whole training sessions. Why had she told Fletcher that she'd search for the Myricals alone? All those weeks of searching together – it had seemed like such a chore but without it there was a great big hole.

A light drizzle began to fall, adding beads of water to her hair. She looked up hopefully, but the rain was falling widely – on to the path, the grass and on to Hobbin Forest just a few strides away – so she couldn't possibly have made it happen. She gazed at the edge of the wood, wondering if she should just go home. There were three trees grouped together straight in front of her. The middle one was smaller than the others and in the fading light it looked like the shape of a man – a tree-man. She stared idly at it, picking out its features. The top branches looked like arms and there was a knobbly bulge for its head. The leaves gave the tree-man a sort of coat down to its trunk-like legs.

A meow came from behind her and she jumped up. "Dizzy! Don't creep up on me like that!"

The little black cat paced up and down, uttering a string of meows.

"I'm sorry, I don't know what you're saying." Laney leaned over to pet her, but Dizzy bared her teeth and darted back into the bushes. "Suit yourself then. I was only going to stroke you." She was talking to cats now, like Claudia.

She glanced back at the trees again. But this time something was missing – as if someone had reached down with a giant hand and plucked an object out of the scene. Her mind spun. What was it – what had changed? Then she realised the tree that looked like a man had gone and now there was a gap where it had been.

For a few seconds, she couldn't pull her eyes away. Then she ran.

When Laney got home she decided to tell her dad that she'd been expelled from training. Then he wouldn't be shocked when Frogley spoke to him the next day.

"Well, you know I was never that keen on the idea anyway," he said. "Being a close member of a tribe does funny things to people. They forget who they really are – where the tribe ends and they begin. Who was it that got you into trouble?"

"Jessie Weir," said Laney.

"Oh yes, I know her mum. She's had a hard time since her husband went. Aren't you about the same age as Jessie?"

Laney didn't want to talk about Jessie. "Yeah, about the same. Dad, did you know there are some ruined buildings at the bottom of Faymere Lake?"

Mr Rivers blinked. "Yes, I knew. Did you go down there?" His voice sounded odd.

"We all did. We were practising underwater flying. I never realised the lake was so deep." Footsteps came down the stairs and Kim walked in before she could ask any more.

"Laney, you need to get to bed. It's school tomorrow," said Kim. "Here, I've filled in the form about your geography field trip."

"Thanks." Laney took the form.

"Where are you going on this field trip?" said her dad, slipping back into his normal tone.

"To the river – we're collecting soil samples and stuff," said Laney. "Last year they got people to go into the water but this year we can't because of the flood. They think it might be too deep."

"Perhaps your teacher can figure out why it suddenly flooded here when there's never been a problem before," said Kim. "The council doesn't seem to have a clue. I feel sorry for Simon living down on Silverbrook Close. If the river bursts its banks again he'll be one of the first to be flooded."

Laney decided to leave them to their conversation and started to go up the stairs. As she reached the top, she heard her dad say in a low voice, "That's another good reason to think about moving away from Skellmore. We don't want to be caught out by a flood like that again."

Laney heard Kim sigh, and then came the rustle of her dad's newspaper, as if that meant an end to the discussion. She shut her bedroom door behind her, glad to get away from all the secrets floating round the downstairs room.

CHAPTER
13

The end of September slipped closer, but the sun stayed bright and the leaves on the trees grew as thick and green as they did in mid-summer. Laney wondered if she should go and talk to Gwen about the moving tree roots in Hobbin Forest and her suspicions about Stingwood. It had been nearly a month since her accident with the Spirit Smoke – surely Gwen would have forgiven her by now.

But when at last she went over to Gnarlwood Lane, she found Stingwood striding up Gwen's front path. He went into the house and came out an hour later, pausing to look around and scowling as if he suspected that someone was spying on him. Laney stayed hidden behind the hedge and was too nervous to knock on the door even after he'd gone. Every time she passed Gwen's house after that there was strange-coloured smoke wafting from the trumpet-shaped flowers on the roof. Laney felt like the smoke was a Do Not Disturb sign.

She spent most afternoons Myrical hunting after school or trying to follow Stingwood. She watched him at his house in Gillforth and tracked him to the edge of Hobbin Forest, but once he entered the wood she could never find him. She looked out for the withered plants and brown leaves that signalled the presence of the Shadow but found nothing. Once, from the corner of her eye, she saw a huge black shape skimming over the treetops, but when she turned it was gone.

The day of the geography field trip was warm and bright. Kids piled on to the coaches at Pennington School, and Laney and Steph found a seat together. The year above was also on the trip and Laney spotted Fletcher sitting at the back with his friends.

"Now, listen up!" Their geography teacher, Mrs Martin, stood at the front of the coach. "There's been a change of plan. There's rain forecast for later and we need to be careful about the river just in case it floods like it did in the summer. So we're going to the woods instead. We can still take soil samples and do measurements. I'll give you your worksheets once we get there."

There was a series of groans and cheers, and the coaches set off. Feeling thirsty, Laney pulled out her water bottle. A few bubbles rolled up to the surface as she tipped it up. She drank some and pulled a face. She'd heated the water again. She had to stop doing that – it made it taste horrible. Putting the bottle away quickly, she turned to chat to Steph. When she looked out of the window half an hour later she realised with a jolt that when Mrs Martin had said the woods, she'd actually meant Hobbin Forest.

The coaches parked up in a lay-by opposite

Skellmore Farm and they made their way along the footpath that led to the forest, stopping just before the trees.

"Shouldn't we try another wood, Miss?" said Fletcher. "This one's really easy to get lost in."

"You'll be fine, Fletcher. I'm giving you all a map," said Mrs Martin.

Fletcher tried again. "But, Miss—"

"Right, everyone! Gather round!" bellowed Mrs Martin, and she started giving instructions and handing out sheets and clipboards.

Laney saw Fletcher's worried face. She was still annoyed with him, but she understood what he was trying to do. Hobbin Forest was not a good place for a bunch of school kids right now. The mass of dark trees stretched in front of them, waiting.

"Now, I'll put you into pairs and you can work together, share the map and bring back one set of soil samples and measurements." Mrs Martin began calling out names. "Steph Mackall and Craig Mottle." Steph pulled an agonised face. "Laney Rivers and Fletcher Thornbeam." Laney sighed. She might have known she'd be paired up with Fletcher. She went to collect their map and clipboard, nearly tripping over Jessie, who was doing the same.

"Watch it!" Jessie snatched the nearest clipboard and went back to Cathy and Leah. Laney raised her eyebrows, wondering how Jessie had managed to end up in a group with her friends.

"Spread out and find different places to take measurements but be back here by three o'clock," Mrs Martin called. "The coach won't wait."

"Here you are." Laney handed the map to Fletcher and picked up the soil sample bags and the clipboard. Then they walked into the wood in silence.

"Are you still annoyed with me?" said Fletcher at last. "I can't even remember what I said that upset you."

Laney stuck her hands in her pockets. "You were freaked out that I got those roots off Craig when you couldn't do it."

"It *was* kind of strange. Maybe Mist power is stronger than I thought."

"You don't think I'm out of control then?"

Fletcher pulled a face. "I'm sorry I said that. Look – you've only just started your Mist training. You've got years to practise and learn how to handle your powers. Let's just forget it and get this worksheet done."

Laney hesitated. "Actually, I won't be having any more Mist training. Frogley told me not to come back any more. It wasn't my fault," she added quickly. "Jessie set me up. I guess she can be happy now that she's the only proper Mist kid in Skellmore again."

"That sucks! She shouldn't have done that."

"Yeah – well. That's Jessie." Laney scooped up some loose earth and put it in one of the plastic bags. "OK, here's the first soil sample."

"Made up then, have you?" came a voice from above them.

Laney jerked in surprise, hitting her head on a branch. Claudia was perched halfway up a beech tree, swinging her legs. "Claudia! Don't sneak up on us like that! What have you done with your partner?"

"I got rid of her," Claudia said casually. "She went off with her friends. I persuaded her to go with them actually. She was pretty easy to convince. Then I came to find you – there's no way I'm going round this place with only humans for protection after what happened the last time we were here. We virtually got strangled by tree roots!" She inspected the ground below, as if expecting the roots to spring up at any moment.

"It wasn't quite that bad," said Fletcher. "And it was Craig who got trapped by them, not you."

"Still, I'm not taking any chances," said Claudia. "At least together we have a range of skills against *the evil trees.*" She dropped her voice to a whisper.

"If they're so evil why are you sitting on one?" Fletcher asked.

"Mrs Martin will tell you off if she finds out you've

ditched your partner," said Laney.

Claudia jumped down, landing softly on the earth. "Oh, who cares? Old Martin's always moaning about something. The worst she can do is give me detention. She doesn't know what she's done – bringing us here."

"I wish she'd stuck to taking us to the river," said Fletcher. "The forest doesn't want us here, I can feel it."

"I told you." Claudia widened her eyes in a theatrical manner. "*This* is the forest of doom."

"At least we can do some Myrical hunting. I've got the adder stone here." Laney took the stone out of her pocket. "We can search a little bit in between doing the measurements."

"Put that away!" said Fletcher. "Someone will see it."

A group of kids came past, talking loudly. Craig had somehow managed to team up with Jack Turney, even though they weren't supposed to be partners. Steph dragged along behind them, looking cross. She saw Laney and rolled her eyes, pointing at Craig.

"Flippin' hell!" Craig shouted to Jack. "Steph got freaked out just now cos she thought a tree moved! Maybe that means this place is haunted."

Laney turned cold. She remembered the strange man-like tree that had vanished on the day Frogley had expelled her from Mist training. "What if something's starting?" she said to Fletcher and Claudia. "We rescued Craig that time but we can't rescue a hundred people from this forest."

"Maybe we can keep the humans out of the most dangerous part of the wood," said Fletcher. "I know a barrier enchantment. It's a beginner spell but it works for a little while on humans."

"If this is Stingwood's secret project, then we should definitely keep *away* from it," said Claudia, pausing at the top of a steep wooded slope. "Why are we always walking into trouble? It's not normal."

"Over here – this is the direction they came from." Fletcher hurried down the hill, followed by Claudia, who was still muttering.

Laney dropped her pen halfway down the slope and crouched down, trying to find it among the fallen leaves. Claudia and Fletcher got to the bottom and ran on. Laney felt the long plastic shape of the pen under the leaves and grabbed it. She put the school clipboard under one arm and shoved the pen in her pocket. She was still carrying the soil sample and the adder stone too. She wished she'd made Fletcher take some of this stuff. Stopping for a moment, she tried to wedge the plastic sample bag into her other pocket when something made her look up.

There was a stunted tree at the top of the hill.

They must have passed it on the way down. Heavy branches stretched upwards, forming a terrible twisted shape, and the sparse leaves looked strange, as if they were growing where leaves were never meant to be. There was a series of bumps near the top of the trunk – a knotted shape that looked almost like a face. Laney recognised the contorted features. It was the tree-man she'd seen when she'd left Mist training – the one that had disappeared when she wasn't looking.

She turned to tell the others but they were too far away. Somehow she didn't want to shout for them, just in case something was listening. . .

The twisted branches jerked sideways and Laney threw herself on to the ground. There was no wind and the branches of the other trees were completely still, but she knew the stunted tree had moved. As she watched, the branches began to shake harder and harder until great convulsions ran through the whole tree. The craggy brown face on the tree trunk crumpled. Ruts in the tree bark grew deeper and a mouth formed from a hollow in the trunk – a tree-like mouth with wooden teeth. A knobble above the mouth moulded into a protruding nose. Then, at the top, two pale gashes grew wider and wider.

The tree opened its eyes and looked around.

CHAPTER

14

Laney kept her head low, praying that the tree thing hadn't seen her – praying that she was far enough down the slope to be hidden.

The tree-man moaned and shook his arms. Leaves fell. The whole trunk shuddered and gradually the tree warmed from green-brown to a human colour, as if a child was shading in its body with a felt-tip.

"Stifle with stems. Bind with roots. Deep in the earth," rumbled the tree in a voice just like Stingwood's. The bottom of the trunk became two long legs and one of the branches became a walking stick. The broad-framed man wrenched his feet from the ground, breaking free from tangled roots and showering the place with earth.

Laney stared. It *was* Stingwood. She could hardly believe it.

"No! There's no time for this!" Stingwood growled, kicking the roots that were still trying to cling to his feet. "Release me! I have important things to do!" He lumbered away through the forest, still shedding leaves from his clothes and hair.

Laney raced through the trees, nearly colliding with Fletcher. "I've just seen Stingwood," she gasped. "He changed from a tree to a man. He was actually a tree to start with."

"No way! Was it an *evil* kind of tree?" said Claudia.

Fletcher made a face. "You don't get evil trees.

Trees are full of sacred energy – they're the purest things on this planet."

Claudia snorted.

"Do you get trees that turn into faeries?" asked Laney. "Because that's what just happened."

"It must have been a really good camouflage spell." Fletcher began walking back up the slope.

"It wasn't camouflage! He was *actually* a tree – I saw his branches and his face was like bark!" Laney realised she was shouting and dropped her voice. "I'll find him and prove it."

"Calm down. You'll have Mrs Martin on our case," Fletcher said maddeningly. "I'm sure you thought you saw Stingwood as a tree but it must have been a disguise. Transformation spells aren't a normal part of Thorn magic."

Laney's hands grew hot and her palms itched. "I know what I saw."

"I'll help you find him, Water Girl," said Claudia suddenly. "I can track him."

"It's a waste of time," said Fletcher. "And it could be dangerous."

But the girls ignored him, and Fletcher sighed as he followed after them. Claudia led the way, listening for Stingwood's movements and following his scent through the wood. The sky darkened as heavy rain clouds closed in and the leaves on every tree began fluttering in unison, filling the air with their rushing noise.

"It sounds like a warning," said Laney nervously.

"But is it warning us or warning him?" said Claudia.

They crossed a forest stream and waded through patches of brambles. All traces of the other kids faded behind them. Laney caught sight of Stingwood's bulky frame up ahead. Claudia held up a hand and they stopped.

"He doesn't look much like a tree to me," muttered Fletcher.

Laney ignored him. A tumbling feeling in her stomach told her that something was about to happen. Something big.

Stingwood paused at the top of a long avenue of silver birch trees set apart from the rest of the forest. He rested on his walking stick and his massive shoulders rose up and down, as if he were taking deep breaths. Then he strode forward between the two long lines of trees. Halfway down, he began to fade into a translucent ghost-like shape. Then he vanished completely.

"Is he invisible?" Claudia looked nervous. "I don't like this. He could sneak up on us."

"Thorns can't turn invisible," said Fletcher.

"Yeah, just like they can't turn into trees," said Claudia. "Maybe you don't know as much as you think, Twig Boy."

"Guys! This is it!" cried Laney. "Don't you recognise that avenue of trees?"

"Course I do!" Fletcher said. "We saw this place in the Spirit Smoke. That enormous Thorn Elder walked through here carrying the Wildwood Arrow."

"Why didn't you tell us about this place before then?" said Claudia. "I thought you knew every bit of the forest."

"This isn't usually here. These lines of silver birches have been brought here magically." He turned to Laney. "Quick – have you got the adder stone? Get it out! Check for the spell shimmer."

"I still think we should be checking that there's no invisible Stingwood lurking around," grumbled Claudia.

Laney groped in her pocket for the stone. Holding it up to her eye, she saw an unmistakable trembling in the air. She'd never seen spell shimmer before but this had to be what they were looking for.

"Let's see!" said Claudia, and Laney handed it over. "Whoa! That is . . . really shimmery."

"Then we've found a Myrical – finally!" said Laney.

"Yeah, but which one?" Claudia folded her arms. "We can't just assume it'll be the Arrow."

"It has to be because we saw the Thorn Elder here in the Spirit Smoke. It's all the same!" Fletcher took his turn at looking through the adder stone, his face glowing. "I can't believe it – the Arrow! The things we can do with it! It's meant to possess the power to heal any plant – even bring dead ones back to life. We'll be able to transform the countryside. Make things green again!"

"I assume when you say *we*, you mean you and the other Thorns," said Claudia.

"Don't forget what we really have to do." Laney pushed her wispy hair away from her face. "We've got to find the Arrow and lock it away like we did with the Crystal Mirror. We can't go off round the countryside healing stuff. I bet the Shadow would like to use the Arrow for a few things too."

Fletcher's face dropped. "I know we're trying to keep the Myricals safe. But the Wildwood Arrow is full of good, pure Thorn power. It won't hurt people."

"Well, the Crystal Mirror wasn't exactly nasty either." Laney felt her hands grow hotter and hid them behind her back. "Let's just find the Arrow, OK?"

Fletcher walked to the head of the silver birch avenue. "I should be able to feel where the Arrow is because of the pull of Thorn magic."

"Then once you've found it you've just got to get it away from Stingwood," said Claudia drily. "I'm sure he'll be really pleased to share."

"Shh! I have to concentrate." Fletcher took a tentative step forwards.

"Stingwood must know it's here," muttered Laney. "Especially if he's. . ." She and Claudia exchanged a look. *If Stingwood is the Shadow. . .*

Fletcher took another step.

"Oh, come on!" Claudia sprang past him down the avenue of trees. Halfway along, she bounced backwards and tumbled to the ground. She leapt up, glaring round furiously. "What on earth—"

"Wait! Just let me do it. You'll ruin everything!" said Fletcher. "You don't understand Thorn power."

Laney ignored him and went right up to the place where Claudia had fallen over. The avenue of birches stretched on into the distance and everything looked perfectly normal. Not a leaf was out of place and it gave her the odd feeling that she was looking at a painting. She put the adder stone to her eye for a moment. She was really close to the spell shimmer. It was like standing next to a waterfall of light. She put out one hand and came up against an invisible barrier that felt soft and silky.

"There's something here. It's not letting me through." She pressed harder and the wall pushed back. "It's really strong . . . but soft too."

Fletcher reached out till he felt the wall and then pushed against it. "Stingwood must have gone right through." He stepped closer. "I can see something.

A whole different wood with an outcrop of rock in the middle and it's covered in birches like a tower of trees. It's so bright . . . it's a perfect forest."

Claudia came over, squinting hard. "All I can see is the two lines of trees. Why can't I see what you're seeing?" She crowded closer to Fletcher, bumping his shoulder. "Oh! It's there!" She stepped back, before taking hold of his arm.

"What are you doing?" He shook her off.

I can only see it when I'm touching you," Claudia told him. "It's like a blindfold comes off."

Laney grasped Fletcher's other arm and leaned forwards. The scene clouded over and then cleared to show exactly what Fletcher had described: a wood more alive than any she'd ever seen and a crown of trees on a rocky outcrop. Even she, a Mist faerie, could feel the dream-like pull of the place. "It's full of Thorn magic."

"It's the most Thorn-tastic place I've ever seen," Claudia agreed. "Amazing, in a mad sort of way."

"The Wildwood Arrow has to be in there somewhere." Laney pressed her face right up to the invisible wall and felt it push back.

"I bet it's on that rock in the middle," said Claudia. "I mean, look at it – the trees and everything. It just reeks of power."

"That's Spine Tree Ridge. My dad told me about it. It's where Stingwood's building his Avalon project."

Fletcher pushed hard against the barrier with his shoulder.

"You won't break in." Claudia tapped the wall with a fingernail. "This is completely solid."

"I have to get in," Fletcher said. "I have to find the Arrow."

Laney put her hand on Fletcher's shoulder to take another look at the hidden wood. The trees inside were flawless, coloured in glowing greens and yellows. The grey clouds stopped at the barrier and the sky inside was bright blue. Fletcher seemed hypnotised, his hands resting on the invisible wall.

"We should go back," said Claudia suddenly. "We need to be back on that coach at three. I'd rather tell Gwen about this place than try to get in."

"I'm not going." Fletcher stared longingly at the wood.

"We have to," Laney told him, then paused. Beyond the invisible wall, black tree roots rose from the ground like snakes. Earth showered in all directions. "Did you see that? The roots are moving on that side of the wall too."

The black roots twisted across the ground and when they passed close to a tree, a wave of dark colour rushed up its trunk.

"Oi! What are you doing?"

Laney spun round. Two Greytails stood at the entrance to the birch avenue. One was Claudia's brother, Tom; the other was his friend Charlie Springer.

"We're here on a school trip," said Claudia. "What are *you* doing?"

Tom frowned and Laney wondered what had happened to the cheeky Tom that always used to tease her. "We're wasting time," he told Charlie. "Leave them – we'll start further along." A tortoiseshell cat dashed out of the trees and stood by his legs.

"But your sister's hanging out with a Thorn," said Charlie.

"Yeah," Tom said. "But she's on a school trip so she can't help it, can she?"

"What's your problem?" Claudia said fiercely.

"My problem is that none of you should be here," replied Charlie.

"No, *you* shouldn't be here!" Fletcher bristled. "This is a Thorn place and Greytails should stay out." He caught Claudia glaring at him. "I didn't mean you!"

"Don't lump us all together then!" said Claudia.

"I wasn't, I—" Fletcher's eyes swivelled to a clump of bushes that were rustling and shaking. "How many cats have you got in there?"

"A few," Tom said. A crow landed on a silver birch and turned its beady eye on Fletcher. "Some birds too."

"You're nosing around," snapped Fletcher. "You're setting up spies to find out what's going on." The tortoiseshell cat turned its eyes on him, unblinking.

"We know about your Avalon project – we knew ages ago," Tom said. "We told our Elders but everything went quiet and they decided the project wasn't a threat any more. But we knew you Thorns would start it up again when you thought no one was looking. What you're doing is dangerous – one of the cats only just escaped injury yesterday. And what happens after Saturn Rising?"

"What's Saturn Rising?" Laney asked.

Fletcher ignored her. "You can't come here," he told the older boys. "You're nosing into Thorn business."

Laney was about to ask about the Saturn thing again when she felt the invisible wall tremble behind her and heard Tom's friend give a shout. The two Greytails changed instantly to faerie form and rose into the air.

"Claudia! Laney! Get down!" Tom yelled.

Laney turned and a bolt of white lightning zapped past her ear. Stingwood loomed up, his tree-like features gone. He cast down his walking stick and aimed a barrage of lightning at them with his huge hands.

CHAPTER 15

Claudia pulled Laney to the ground as streams of electricity rippled through the air. The Greytails swooped out of the way before shooting lightning back.

Laney's head pulsed with the crackling of the bolts. She hadn't known Tom could make lightning. Usually you didn't learn that until you were an adult and she knew Tom was only seventeen.

"Stop! Everyone stop!" Fletcher stepped in front of Stingwood. "We're not here to spoil anything or get in your way, we just—"

"But you *are* in my way and now you must move." Stingwood pointed his walking stick at Fletcher for a moment. Then his stony face softened as he gazed back through the invisible wall. "I'm so close now," he muttered. "So close to making Avalon a place of unrivalled natural beauty."

"Did you use anything special to make it?" said Fletcher. "I mean—"

"It's all special!" Stingwood growled. "Imagine a place with no humans, no chemicals in the air, no poisoned water . . . all of it perfect without a single blemish." He glared at Laney and Claudia, his eyes wild. "And then you stroll up with Mist trash and a Filthy Tail to infect the place. It's an abomination! Get them out of here!" He advanced on the girls.

Fletcher stood his ground but Stingwood knocked him aside as if he was swatting a fly. The

Thorn boy fell to the earth, groaning.

"Fletcher!" Laney cried, crawling towards him.

"Picking on your own tribe now, Stingwood?" yelled Tom, flying straight at him. "That shows how low you've sunk."

"Stay out of this forest, Greytails," roared Stingwood. "Your kind doesn't belong here." He shot more lightning at them.

Laney reached Fletcher and fear twisted inside her when she saw how still and pale he was. She took hold of his arm and he groaned again.

Stingwood advanced, letting loose great volleys of lightning. Tom and Charlie shot back, firing short bursts from their fingertips but Stingwood's bolts were stronger and the Greytails fell back. Stingwood's lightning intensified and he fired without stopping, his mouth twisting horribly.

Lightning flew over Laney's head as she crouched low by Fletcher. Tom and Charlie's attack bolts were stuttering now. Laney let go of Fletcher's arm and clasped her hands together, willing her Mist power to work – wishing for water to burst from the earth and wash Stingwood away. None came.

"Get out of here, Tom!" Claudia yelled. "Just go!"

Stingwood spun round and threw lightning at her. Laney watched her dodge behind a tree. Her heart pounded. She and Claudia could transform and fly away but they couldn't leave Fletcher.

Charlie cried out as a lightning bolt hit his leg. The barrage of spells ceased. Laney looked up hopefully, but she could see from Stingwood's face that he was preparing for an all-out attack.

She pointed all her fingers at the sky the way the older Mist faeries did. *Let it rain. Bring the storm.* Her hands throbbed painfully. But Stingwood saw what she was doing and crossed to her in a few strides.

"The Mists had better stay out of my forest too," he roared. "And you – you bring disaster wherever you go." He snatched her outstretched hands and pulled them down to her sides.

Laney tensed, waiting for the lightning strike but instead she felt something soft brush past her ankle. A stream of cats poured out of the woods and Tom and Charlie shouted to them, egging them on. They swept past Laney and leapt on Stingwood, biting and scratching every piece of skin they could find.

Stingwood shot off another bolt of lightning but he was pulled off balance by the cats clinging to his arms and legs, and the bolt zapped uselessly into the ground.

"Call the cats off!" Claudia shouted to her brother. "Call them off. He'll hurt them."

Laney knelt down by Fletcher and shook him. "Come on – wake up!" She hated seeing him like this, with his eyes closed and his skin so pale.

"Wake up, Fletcher!" She shook him again, and he moaned and opened his eyes.

Stingwood's face darkened and black roots sprang from the ground, twisting into the air to catch hold of the cats.

"Get back! Retreat!" Tom yelled, and the cats jumped away from the Thorn Elder, who was staggering around wildly. He had a deep diagonal gash on his cheek and something was oozing from it. He wiped his face on his arm, leaving a dark-green bloodstain on his sleeve. Laney stared, horrified, at the strange-coloured blood.

A large ginger tom pounced on one of the black roots, shredding it with his claws and Stingwood howled with fury.

"Fletcher, we have to get you out of here." Laney hitched his arm over her shoulder and helped him to stand. He swayed woozily. She pulled him forward, supporting his weight, and Claudia ran to take his other arm.

"Can you switch form?" Laney asked him. "It'll be easier to fly you out of here if you've changed."

"Uh . . . maybe. . ." Fletcher closed his eyes and managed to transform.

Laney and Claudia changed to faerie form too, and dragged him into the air. A lightning bolt crackled past Laney's leg. She turned and saw the cats streaming away into the forest.

"Get out of here, Claudia! We'll hold him off," shouted Tom, swooping over the birch avenue. "And don't tell Mum about this when you get home!"

Stingwood's lightning bolts began to stutter and his arms looked stiff and angular. Leaves fluttered where his fingers had been. Long creases formed on his face giving him a tortured look. "No!" he cried out. "Make it stop."

"Look at him," coughed Fletcher. "You were right, Laney. He's becoming a tree."

Stingwood roared as his face turned to tree bark, and the roar became the creaking of branches.

"Just hold on." Laney beat her wings grimly, desperate to get higher in case Stingwood managed to shoot more lightning.

Fletcher hung between her and Claudia, his wings drooping. They flew away from the birch avenue, and Laney darted one last look at the crooked figure of Stingwood stretching his branch-arms up to the sky.

Laney and Claudia glided over the forest, pulling Fletcher between them. Laney looked around for some sign of where they were. The treetops spread below in all directions. "We need to get out of the sky. If someone down there is walking their dog or something we'll be seen in a heartbeat."

"Not to mention the hundred or so kids on the field trip that are loose in this forest," added Claudia.

They flew down. Supporting Fletcher at the same time as landing was difficult and they ended up collapsing on the leaf-strewn ground.

"If the Elders find out we flew while we were on a school trip they are going to be so mad," said Laney.

"Getting grounded will have a whole new meaning," agreed Claudia.

Fletcher clutched his stomach, grimacing. "Don't you think they're going to be more interested in the news that Stingwood attacked us, and that Tom and Charlie used lightning spells even though they're not eighteen yet."

Laney pushed her hair out of her eyes. "The Wildwood Arrow is in that Avalon place producing all the power. I just—" She broke off, her head jumbled with thoughts. "I've been thinking Stingwood is the Shadow for weeks, but now . . . the way he turned into a tree and the lightning he used. . ."

"It wasn't the red lightning that the Shadow used," Claudia finished off. "I noticed that too. I'll never forget that red lightning."

Beep, beep! The noise of a horn broke through the trees.

Claudia checked her watch. "It's three fifteen! We're already quarter of an hour late for the bus."

"That's why there weren't hordes of kids around as we landed then," said Laney.

Changing into human form, they headed back as fast as they could. Mrs Martin stood by the coach steps with a face like thunder. "Where are your clipboards, maps and samples?"

Laney looked at the others. None of them had anything.

"Get on!" snapped Mrs Martin. "I'll speak to you three when we get back to school."

They made their way to the spare seats halfway down the bus. Laney caught sight of Steph; her eyes were red-rimmed. Jessie was at the back with Cathy and Leah, and she smirked when she saw Laney and muttered something to the others.

As the bus moved off, Laney twisted round to ask Steph if she was all right but Craig's face popped out from the seat behind her. "Steph twisted her ankle," he announced loudly. "And she reckons the tree roots moved to trip her up – says she saw them do it." He drew circles in the air next to his head. "Loopy or what!"

An image of Craig all tied up by tree roots popped into Laney's head and she hid a grin. "Sometimes I wish he remembered how we had to rescue him," she whispered to Claudia.

"Sometimes I wish we'd just left him there," her friend replied.

CHAPTER
16

Laney, Claudia and Fletcher were given two weeks of lunchtime detentions by Mrs Martin, despite pleading that they'd got lost and accidentally left their clipboards behind while trying to work out which way to go. Laney went to look for Steph and found her limping out of school on her injured ankle.

"Oh, you remember me then," Steph said accusingly. "I thought you were too busy hanging out with your new friends."

"Yeah, if you call being told off by Mrs Martin 'hanging out'," Laney said. "Is your ankle really bad?"

"I can walk on it a bit better now. It's going to take me a while to get home though."

"Can't you call your mum and get a lift?" Laney's gaze twisted upwards, her eyes drawn to a cloud of silvery sprites flying over the school roof. It was really strange to see them here. She still wasn't used to the faerie world colliding with school.

"She'll be busy at work." Steph scanned her friend's face closely. "You seem kind of different lately. I'm not sure you're listening to me half the time."

"I was listening." Laney pulled her gaze away from the sprites.

The school bus started its engine. Steph gave a half-smile. "You'd better go. You're going to miss the bus."

"I'll phone you later." Laney ran for the bus, getting on just before it pulled away. She sat down next to Fletcher, braving the glares of the other Thorns. "Do you feel OK?" she asked quietly.

"My ribs are a bit sore but it's no big deal. I just want to get back and tell my dad what we saw." Fletcher lowered his voice. "I can't believe the Wildwood Arrow's inside that Avalon place, just waiting to be found."

"We have to work out how to get past the invisible wall first." Laney wasn't sure it was as simple as Fletcher was saying. "We should talk to Gwen straight away. She didn't want other people knowing about the Myrical search in case it helped . . . y'know . . . the Shadow." She caught sight of Fletcher's expression. "I don't mean your dad would plan to do that." She changed the subject hastily. "Fletch, what's Saturn Rising? Tom said *what happens after Saturn Rising*, like it was something that would make everything worse."

"It's a thing, an occasion really, that the tribes have." His gold-ringed eyes flicked round the bus but no one was listening.

"What happens?"

"Every two and a half years, at the exact moment the sun sets, the planet Saturn rises from behind it. It looks amazing, and most of us feel an increase in

power. The next one's coming up this weekend. . ."
He fell silent as two girls moved seats to sit in front
of them.

The bus drew into Skellmore and stopped
behind a delivery lorry that was parked outside the
minimart. They got off and made their way round
crates of tissues and washing-up liquid that were
being wheeled into the shop. Then Fletcher made
off down Gnarlwood Lane without waiting for
anyone.

"He's moving pretty fast for someone with an
injury," said Laney.

"Thorns always heal fast." Claudia sped up. "He's
going to blab it all to his family, isn't he?"

Laney quickened her pace too. "It's because it's the
Thorn Myrical. That's why he wants to tell them."

"It doesn't matter which Myrical it is!" Claudia
said. "The Shadow could be waiting for something
like this – for someone to let a secret slip. You've
got to stop him. He listens to you."

"Not always." Laney broke into a half-run.
She rounded the corner and found her dad's van
right in front of her. Simon's head poked out of a
manhole and he grinned cheekily. "Watch out!
We don't want you falling in!"

"Thanks, Simon." Laney edged round the hole
with one eye on Fletcher, who was still heading
straight for his house.

Simon picked up a wrench and wiped his forehead. "Your mate's in a hurry, isn't he?"

"Yeah," said Laney, wondering why grown-ups always had to say what was obvious.

Claudia passed them. "Come on, Laney!"

Laney said a hurried goodbye to Simon and ran on down the street. There was no smoke rising from the trumpet-shaped flowers on Gwen's roof and no lights on inside.

Fletcher had reached his front gate. "Fletcher!" called Laney, but he didn't turn round.

"He's not going to listen," said Claudia, turning into Gwen's front garden. "Gwen will know what to do."

The path to Gwen's front door was overgrown with a sea of tiny white flowers floating on tall stems. As they waded through them, a strong scent rose into the air and Laney's head whirled.

Claudia knocked and the girls waited impatiently for the door to open.

"Laney, Claudia!" Gwen smiled at them. Her white hair curled over her wrinkled forehead. Laney thought she looked very strange without a hat.

"Can we come in?" said Claudia. "It's really important."

"Of course." Gwen let them in. "Come this way, I was just . . . I was just. . ." Her brow creased more deeply. "I'm sorry, I'm not sure what I'm saying. Come on in."

The girls exchanged looks and followed Gwen as she walked slowly through the front room and down the corridor to the plant house. A large silver watering can stood in the middle of the floor, and Gwen picked it up and began watering the plants. A clump of roses swayed extravagantly as the water poured all over them. Laney thought they would have sung if they could.

"What can I do for you?" said Gwen.

"Well, it's sort of good and bad news really." Laney paused. The strong scent in the room reminded her of the little white flowers growing in the front garden.

"The good part is we think we've found a Myrical!" Claudia brushed off a vine that was curling over her arm. "But the bad part is that Stingwood's found it too."

Gwen stopped watering and fixed her gaze on them. "Girls, do you know what you're saying? The Myricals were lost thirteen years ago. The tribes searched and searched but no one's ever found them."

"But. . ." Laney faltered. "The Crystal Mirror was found a few months ago and you said we should let you know if we found any more. We're not sure if Stingwood knows he's close to the Wildwood

Arrow. But he's working on a secret project in Hobbin Forest – making an area for Thorns that humans can't enter called the Avalon project. That's what Fletcher's dad says, and we saw the place today but we couldn't get in."

"Then Stingwood came along and attacked us with lightning spells," said Claudia.

Gwen blinked and picked up the watering can again. "This is a lot to take in, girls." She sounded stern. "You'd better slow down and explain it to me properly. Ah, just one moment. This is empty." She peered into the watering can, then took it over to the tap and began filling it with water.

Laney waited, anxiety bubbling in her stomach. Claudia flicked a leaf impatiently with her finger and it curled itself up into a ball.

Gwen turned back to them, her watering can full. "Now, girls, what did you want to talk to me about?" She smiled, her face serene.

Laney's eyebrows rose. "Well, about Stingwood and the Myrical – I don't think we really explained it very well."

"Explained what, dear?" said Gwen.

The flowery scent grew, making Laney feel dizzy. "Remember what we just said about the Myrical? It's just that—" she coughed.

"Start at the beginning, dear." Gwen started pouring water on to the clump of roses.

"You've already watered those roses," said Claudia suddenly.

Gwen laughed. "I can't have done. I've only just filled up the watering can."

Laney drew her breath in sharply. She beckoned Claudia over to a corner. "It's like she's forgotten the whole conversation. Why doesn't she remember anything?"

"It could be a spell," said Claudia tightly. "She doesn't seem to remember anything about finding the Myricals either."

Gwen walked over to a small lemon tree and began watering it. "Hello, girls," she said suddenly. "How are you? I didn't see you come in."

Tears sprang to Laney's eyes. "Someone's done this to her," she whispered.

"How can they? Gwen's more powerful than any other faerie I know," said Claudia.

"Yeah maybe . . . except for one person." Laney pictured the dark figure of the Shadow.

"Use the adder stone! If someone's enchanted her we might be able to see a spell shimmer around her."

Laney felt in her pocket. "I haven't got it. I gave it to Fletcher when we were in the woods. He must still have it." She looked over at Gwen. "If this *is* a spell she won't be able to help us. We'll have to find the Arrow on our own and get it to safety."

"We could try breaking the spell," said Claudia. "Although that's going to be hard if we don't know what it is."

Laney turned back up the passageway. "Do you think the air feels funny in here – sort of thick?"

"There's a horrible flowery smell." Claudia glanced into the kitchen as they passed. "Look, she's left something for you."

On the kitchen worktop there was an open envelope with *Laney* written on it in Gwen's spidery writing. A pen and a sheet of paper lay next to it but the paper was blank.

"That's weird." Laney turned the paper over. It was blank on the other side too.

"Why would she need to write to you?" said Claudia.

"I don't know." Laney turned the envelope over and pulled a piece of paper out of it. This one was covered in writing.

"*Dear Laney*," she read. "*I must write down my thoughts while I still can. I may not be able to do so for much longer and there is much to tell you. I realise there is a risk that these words may be seen by the wrong person but I have to take that chance. I have detected an enchantment at work in this house. I can smell the valerian in every room and it has been strengthening steadily despite my best efforts to banish it. Valerian affects the memory and already I* find myself struggling to remember what I should be writing. I will try to be brief.

For several weeks I have been working on a spell to uncover the true identity of the Shadow. I have become more and more convinced that he or she is someone within our community. At times I have come close, maybe too close, but I have not yet been able to finish the spell. I have kept you at a distance these past few weeks and that is because I didn't want you involved if the spell went wrong.

Do not trust anyone. As yet we don't even know which tribe the Shadow originally came from. My thoughts grow weaker (the paper was smudged, as if her pen had slipped), so I must finish and send this now. Do not come to my house to try to release me from the cage of this enchantment and do not ask anyone else to do so. A curse this strong may have defences built into it that could place you in grave peril. You must concentrate on the search for the Myricals.

If you find a Myrical, do not hesitate. Put it through the hole in the Mencladden Stone just as we did with the Crystal Mirror. Remember you will need a faerie from the correct tribe to put it through. The next Myrical will be safe inside Time just as the Mirror is, but the spell cannot be extended. The date was set for a year and a day when we hid the Mirror. As I write I cannot remember what date that was. I trust you *will remember."*

Laney took a deep breath and read on. "*I have one more thing to tell you. Your Mist Elder, Mr Frogley, spoke to me about your performance during training and he tells me your power displays certain qualities. I know this must be difficult for you, but*"

The sentence was left unfinished and the rest of the page was blank. Laney turned it over, but the other side was blank too. Gwen must have forgotten what she was about to write. Had she been about to warn Laney, or to tell her off for not controlling her powers?

"It must have been horrible knowing that she was being captured by the spell," said Claudia. "The Shadow must have realised she was close to discovering him and that's why he made the enchantment. Let's go, this is freaking me out."

Laney crumpled the letter into her pocket and looked back at Gwen, who was humming to herself in the plant house. "She doesn't even seem to know what's happening." She picked up a padlocked jar, which stood on the worktop. It was labelled *Moonwort from my plant house: picked on July 15th this year.* "Hey, that was my birthday – the fifteenth of July." She stared at the label. "There was something else important about that day, but I can't really think. . ."

"The spell's starting to affect you!" said Claudia. "It's in the air – that's why the flowery smell's so extreme. We're breathing in the valerian."

"We need to get rid of the scent and break the enchantment around Gwen," said Laney. "I wish I had wind magic like a Kestrel faerie, then I'd blow the scent away." Rushing back into the plant house, she went to the nearest window and struggled with the catch. Gwen was sitting on the bench, gazing into space. A sudden shaft of sunlight through the glass revealed hundreds of tiny green specks floating in the air like dust.

Laney swung the window open and hurried to the next one. The green dust swirled in the draught. Then something else moved. A patch of darkness shifted on the floor under the bench, slowly gathering into small puddle shapes and seeping outwards. Laney stared, wondering at first if she'd imagined it. "Claudia! Can you see that?"

"That must be the spell defence," Claudia said. "It knows we want to break the enchantment."

The shadows darkened in the corners of the room, underneath the shrubs and leaves, and by the door. They fused together, spreading and swelling like a disease. Then they flowed past Gwen as if she wasn't there, gathering around Laney and Claudia.

Laney's skin prickled. "It's not interested in Gwen. It's just after us. What do you think happens if it touches us?"

"I don't know. We could become caught by the spell, or worse. I don't want to find out," Claudia told her.

Laney edged forwards, seeking the place with the narrowest patch of shadows. Then she leapt over the darkness and ran up the corridor, hearing Claudia running behind her. They bolted through the front door and down the path, through gently swaying stems of little white flowers.

Claudia closed the front gate and leaned on it. "So, next time Gwen tells us we shouldn't mess with something, we don't mess with it, OK?"

Laney wiped her forehead with her hand. "Now she's trapped in there with no power to remember and we can't even ask anyone to help."

"She's strong though. She'll fight it."

Laney reached over the gate to touch one of the little white flowers. *I can smell the valerian in every room*, Gwen had written. Were these the flowers behind the spell? She certainly hadn't seen them growing in Gwen's garden before. Her head whirled as a wave of scent broke over her, forcing her to back away down the lane.

CHAPTER 17

"We need to get back to the forest and we need Fletcher," said Laney. "But he will have told his parents everything by now and they're bound to try to stop us going." She bit her lip. On the corner, her dad and Simon were packing tools into the van. The Thornbeam house stood at the opposite end of the lane. At that moment Fletcher came out of his front door and saw them.

"The Thorns will definitely try to stop us going." Claudia arched her eyebrows. "They'll think that it's their Myrical and nothing to do with anyone else. And as nobody else but us believes in the Shadow, they won't see the danger in talking about it."

"Then all we can do is try to get there first," said Laney. "Fletcher!"

Fletcher came towards them, his shoulders slumped. Before Laney could open her mouth, he started speaking. "So I thought my parents would be thrilled to hear about the Wildwood Arrow, but guess what? They didn't believe me – not about what we saw or anything." He swallowed. "Actually, they laughed."

Claudia and Laney looked at each other and tried not to look relieved.

Fletcher's mouth set into a straight line. "And they say I have to keep away from the Avalon project. There's to be another Thorn tribe meeting about it after Saturn Rising."

"Stuff that!" said Laney. "We're going back there today." She quickly told him the bad news about Gwen, trying to keep her voice steady. "So it's up to us to find the Arrow as soon as we can and take it to the Mencladden Stone," she finished. "We can't rely on her for help. Now we just need to get into the Avalon project."

She saw his gloomy expression and wanted to shake him. "Come on!" she cried. "This is a Thorn thing! There has to be a way in that only a Thorn would know."

"As long as we don't have to turn ourselves into trees," added Claudia.

Fletcher thought for a moment. "There could be something in one of my dad's books that'll help us." He turned back up the lane. "You can come in – my parents are in the greenhouse at the bottom of the garden and Sara's out playing."

Laney had never been inside Fletcher's house. The walls were made from a grainy wood the colour of dark honey, which made her feel like she was inside a hollow tree. Pots of bright daffodils stood on a table in the middle. Laney had never seen daffodils in October but she knew Thorns could make flowers grow whenever they liked.

Her gaze swept round the room and she jumped, seeing a movement in the corner. "Did you see that?"

"See what?" Claudia followed her gaze.

"Something small and dark on the floor."

"Nope, nothing there," said Claudia, "and no one has sharper eyes than a Greytail."

Laney tried to relax. She'd thought for a zillionth of a second that she'd seen one of those black roots from the forest. After everything that had happened, she'd better not start imagining things.

Fletcher went to the bookcase and drew out a battered brown book with *Gardener's Almanac* on the front.

"We're not planting beans," said Claudia.

"The title's just a disguise. It's actually full of Thorn stuff." Fletcher flicked the pages, passing over tables full of numbers and words. "We use these things: times of sunset and moonrise, phases of the moon and positions of constellations."

"Seriously? You actually like that kind of thing?" Claudia raised one eyebrow. "I'm glad I'm not a Thorn."

"So are we," said Fletcher.

Laney looked over his shoulder. "*Offerings for the faerie ring at different phases of the moon*," she read. "What are offerings?"

"They're like gifts," said Fletcher.

Claudia's eyebrow looked like it was stuck halfway up her forehead. "Do you actually do that? Leave stuff next to the rings? I've never noticed anything before."

"You haven't been looking very hard then," said Fletcher shortly. "We only use the rings in the countryside, otherwise humans might notice."

"I don't think I could ever worship the rings. They're too scary." Laney couldn't stop looking at the corner.

Fletcher's mouth twisted. "You wouldn't understand. You were brought up by a human stepmum and you don't know half the things—"

"Fletcher? Are you there?" Mr Thornbeam called from the back garden.

Fletcher closed the book and ran out of the front door. Claudia and Laney followed him and they sprinted down the lane into the yard behind The Old Eagle pub. They found a fence to sit on at the back, screened by a willow tree's drooping branches.

Fletcher looked through the book for ages. "Mistletoe," he said at last, closing the pages.

"What, that stuff people kiss under at Christmas?" said Laney, disgusted.

Fletcher sighed. "I don't know where the kissing thing comes from, but mistletoe is the plant of transitions – it helps you pass from one place to the next. That's what the book says and that must be why it's hung over doorways at Christmas. The humans pick up our ways sometimes but then they get the meaning wrong." He balanced the book on a fence post. "It could be that the invisible wall is like a doorway into Avalon. If I'm right, the mistletoe will help us go through."

"Are you sure it will work?" asked Laney.

"Not totally sure – but it's the only thing in here that comes close to what we need. And, Laney. . ." He frowned. "We should wait till tomorrow night. Tomorrow's Saturday and the moment the sun sets, Saturn will rise. Our power will be stronger after that."

"We can't wait! Gwen's letter said don't hesitate if you find a Myrical," said Laney. "How is some planet going to boost my power anyway?"

"We Greytails don't believe in lots of superstitions," said Claudia, "but Saturn Rising really works. The rings around the planet are connected to the faerie rings somehow, and that makes more power flow in from the Otherworld. Anyway, we have to go – our tribes will notice if we're not there and start to ask all sorts of awkward questions."

"To be honest, I'm not sure I'll be able to get us through that barrier without the extra power," said Fletcher.

Laney clasped her hands together, feeling them grow hot. Claudia and Fletcher hardly ever agreed, so it was difficult to ignore them when they did.

"You should come too," added Claudia. "A new

faerie ring has formed just off Skellmore Edge and we're gathering there to catch the upwelling."

"It'll be hard for her to come if her tribe doesn't want her," said Fletcher.

"I don't think she should miss it," said Claudia.

"Hey, you can talk *to* me – I'm right here!" Laney jumped down from the fence, her face red. "Your Saturn party sounds very nice, but what if your dad tells people what you said to him about the Arrow? If the Shadow finds out he'll go straight to the forest and get there before we do."

A dark expression spread across Fletcher's face. "My dad didn't believe me. He called me an idiot and said that's what comes of running around with other tribes. So I don't think that he's going to tell a whole load of people what I said."

"But he's always been so nice," said Laney. "I can't believe he'd say something like that."

"Believe it," said Fletcher. "Things change. Maybe people change too."

Laney went home with a hollow feeling in her stomach. She was worried that they weren't going straight back to Hobbin Forest to find the Arrow, but something else bothered her too. She'd never seen things get to Fletcher this way. She pictured his face twisting as he told her she wouldn't understand about worshipping the faerie rings, having had a human stepmum. It was true she hadn't grown up learning the customs of the tribes, but he'd never said it so bluntly before.

After dinner she went to the garage to find her dad. He glanced at her briefly as he packed spanners and screwdrivers into his toolbox. "Everything all right, Laney?"

Laney searched for an easy way into what she wanted to ask but couldn't think of one. "You know the tribes? Do you think people ever want to leave their tribe and be . . . something else?" An image of the Shadow rose in her mind.

Mr Rivers straightened up, a pair of pliers in his hand. "Why? What have they done? Has Frogley been bothering you since he sent you away from training?"

"No, nothing's happened. I just . . . wondered if everyone's really as close to their own tribe as they're acting. Maybe some of them really want other things – like getting more power for themselves."

"Most of them would never dare to go against their tribe," he told her. "It's always been that way. You've seen what it's like for me – they won't even speak to me most of the time."

Laney swallowed. He hadn't really understood what she was asking. The Shadow's image faded. "Dad? Have you heard of Saturn Rising?" She curled her hair behind her ear.

"Yes, it's a big occasion. All the tribes go along to some out-of-the-way place to watch Saturn rise, then after that different tribes celebrate in their own way. I think the Mists do twilight lake flying, but I've never taken part." He wiped his forehead on his sleeve. "They don't make so much fuss of it up north where I come from."

"Why not? I thought it gave us some kind of power boost?"

"It does increase the strength of your magic. Though that's not always a good thing, especially around here." He put the pliers into the toolbox and wiped his hands on his jeans.

"So in Longstone, where you used to live, they didn't celebrate the same stuff?" she asked casually. Her dad never talked very much about where he grew up although she knew it was by the sea.

Mr Rivers knelt down by the toolbox, rearranging some of the things inside. "Sometimes there were celebrations but no Thorns live up there and it's the Thorn tribe that have always loved marking events the most. I guess it's in their nature."

"Oh." She'd never thought about different tribes living in different parts of the country, but it made sense. There were no Kestrels or Blazes in Skellmore. "So which tribes live in Longstone then? Everyone except the Thorns?"

"Only Mists and Kestrels. It's a very remote place

– just rocks and the sea, really." His eyes drifted, as if he were picturing it.

Laney tried to imagine him when he was younger but couldn't. "So did you meet Mum there?"

"No, I didn't." Mr Rivers closed the toolbox lid firmly. "I'd better help Kim with the washing up or she'll be pretty fed up with me." He turned round in the doorway and looked at Laney seriously. "Don't go to the Saturn Rising ceremony, love. The tribes round here have a way of turning everything into a disaster. Trust me."

Laney stared at the toolbox after he'd gone. Why hadn't she told her dad about the Shadow? It was true that Gwen had made them promise to keep the Myrical hunt a secret, for everyone's safety. But she knew that wasn't the only reason. There was something that always stopped her – she just didn't know what it was.

She sighed. No matter what he said, there was no way she was missing Saturn Rising.

The red burn mark on the end of her finger prickled and she rubbed it. She couldn't help thinking that if her mum was alive they'd be a normal faerie family and she'd know about every custom and celebration the way her friends did. The thought dropped inside her like a stone sinking in water. She slammed the garage door shut and made her way back to the house in the dark.

CHAPTER 18

Laney woke up thinking of the invisible wall on the edge of Stingwood's Avalon project. The barrier had been so strong. Would something as small as mistletoe break it? She threw on jeans and a T-shirt, wishing she didn't have to wait till the evening to find out.

It was Saturday and she walked down to the minimart on the pretext of buying chocolate but went instead into the yard to look over the fence at Hobbin Forest. The wood seemed quiet, with no sign of autumn-coloured leaves despite the chill in the air. Dread and excitement mixed inside her like a potion. The Wildwood Arrow was in there somewhere – just waiting to be found.

Mr Frogley's bony figure appeared at the edge of the trees and Laney drew back. Where had he come from? Had he walked along the footpath from Faymere Lake or come from inside the forest? She heard a noise behind her and saw Fletcher's dad coming out of the minimart with a newspaper under his arm. Sinking further back under the branches she realised that she mustn't be seen here. If the Shadow saw her watching the forest he would *know*. She waited till both men were out of sight before returning home. Her skin prickled at the thought of her carelessness ruining everything.

As the day went on, a fine mist drifted in from nowhere, turning everything hazy. Watching through the front window, Laney saw that the mist was thickening moment by moment. By teatime she could only just see the wall at the end of the front garden. The lane beyond was a blur. A dark shape moving alongside the wall made her shiver. Then she wondered if it was someone walking over to Skellmore Edge – the mist was a perfect cover for letting the tribes leave the village unseen.

She leaned one hand on the mantelpiece and a bubbling sound interrupted her thoughts. The roses in a vase next to her hand were wilting while the water they stood in boiled steadily. Quickly she looked around, glad that she was alone. She took a deep breath and tried to calm her mind, and the bubbling gradually disappeared. She had to stop doing things like that. One day she would give herself away.

She slipped out of the house half an hour before sunset and walked up Beacon Way. Other figures loomed out of the mist, heading in the same direction, but no one spoke. The mist thinned right after the last house and finally she could see the dark cliffs of Skellmore Edge – a rocky plateau that stretched for several miles. As she climbed the steep slope, a faint wordless singing began somewhere to the left, and her skin prickled. The newly formed faerie ring must be over there. She suddenly wondered exactly how this power surge from the ring was going to work.

Reaching the top, she remembered to avoid the giant footprints carved into the rock. There was a legend that said they were the footprints of a Shadow faerie who fought a battle here decades ago.

The flat hilltop was covered with faeries split into their tribe groups and some of them were already in faerie form. Many of the Greytails were prowling up and down. Tom Lionhart earned stern words from the Thorn tribe when he strayed too close to them. Claudia's mum, Mrs Lionhart, stood at the centre of the Greytails, where she radiated a fierce authority despite being so small. Claudia was hovering just above the ground, her amber wings moving like a dragonfly's. The Thorns stood a short distance from the other tribes, none of them moving or speaking. Laney glanced at Mr Thornbeam and thought his face looked as if it was carved from stone.

The Mists were there too, standing close together as they murmured and cast looks at the other tribes. Now and then one would rise into the air in one smooth movement and then gently float back to the ground. Only Joe Fenworth smiled when he saw Laney; the others glared at her and resumed their furious whispering. Laney kept her head turned away. They needn't think she wanted to be with them – that was the last thing she wanted. She made for the far side of the plateau, hoping to find a place where she could stand alone and unseen. But Frogley left the Mist group and blocked her path. He frowned at her over the top of his half-moon spectacles. "This is a tribe event." He kept his voice low but his bony fingers were clenched. "It's only meant for those *belonging to a tribe*."

"I'm just. . ." Laney pointed to an empty part of the hilltop. She wanted to explain that she wasn't trying to stand with the other Mists but the words stuck in her throat. She tried to skirt round the Elder but Frogley grabbed her wrist. Instantly her hands grew hot. "You can't stop me being here," she hissed.

Frogley's eyes bulged but he let go of her arm.

"I see the Mist tribe are continuing their tradition for tribal unity," said Mrs Lionhart sharply. "Perhaps we could watch Saturn Rising in peace? There's only a few minutes to go now." She raised her arm towards the western horizon.

"Mind your own business!" muttered Frogley, but he let Laney pass. Most of the Mists ignored her, but Laney caught sight of Simon's shocked face. Obviously her dad hadn't told his workmate how bad things had got at her last training session.

She stumbled, knocking into someone. "Sorry," she mumbled, before realising she'd walked into Jessie. The girls' eyes met before Jessie turned away.

Laney carried on, confused. She'd expected to see something else – triumph maybe – but Jessie just looked worried. She glanced back. Jessie's mum was holding on to her daughter with a scrawny arm, her bedraggled hair hanging over her thin shoulders.

"Stand up, Mum," whispered Jessie. "Just for a few minutes." Her mum tried to straighten before slumping against her daughter again.

Laney found an empty place on the hilltop behind the motionless Thorns. The countryside below glowed orange in the light of the setting sun. Little fields spread out in a rectangular pattern, split up by the ribbon-like roads. A patch of mist hung over Skellmore, and smaller patches further afield marked where Gillforth and Pyton lay.

Laney scanned the tribes and swallowed, wrapping her arms round herself to keep off the cold evening air. She felt a movement at her elbow and Fletcher was there.

"Won't your tribe mind you standing with me?" whispered Laney.

Fletcher shrugged. "Not sure I care right now."

Laney flicked a look at where the Thorns were standing as still as statues. Two figures were missing. "Gwen and Stingwood aren't here."

"Stingwood told the tribe that he would stay near a faerie ring in Hobbin Forest. He said he didn't have the time to come up here," said Fletcher in a low voice. "Gwen must be in her house."

Laney thought of Gwen all alone, fighting the memory spell, and stifled a shiver.

"As soon as this is over, we must go straight to the forest to get the you-know-what," muttered Fletcher.

Laney nodded.

The lowest edge of the sun touched the horizon. The tribes fell silent and Laney found that she was holding her breath. Then voices came from below and two strangers climbed up on to the Edge. The man and woman moved with the unmistakable air of Mists, and their short fair hair and identical features made them look like brother and sister. Frogley started forwards and clasped hands with both the visitors. "We didn't know you were coming! Is anything wrong? I mean, it's a great honour to have you here—"

"Our predictions told us that your region will have a particularly strong yield from the rings," said the woman. "We have come to enjoy the advantage of your good fortune. Is this the closest one?" She pointed down the slope.

"Yes, just over here." Frogley led her past the Thorns. "This ring formed very recently and we hope the updraught will allow us all to benefit from a strong boost of magic." He frowned at the silent Thorns, as if they were in the way.

Laney looked over the cliff edge. She could hear the faint singing of the faerie ring again. This time there were words inside the song, words that told that a great wonder was approaching. Laney hunched her shoulders. She didn't know if she could trust a faerie ring completely. She had once crept close to a different ring and it had lured her inwards, promising her a better life beyond.

"Quiet, everyone, please!" called Mrs Lionhart.

"I'm afraid the Greytails here are incredibly bossy," Frogley complained loudly to the Mist visitors. "They find it quite impossible to get along with other tribes."

"We are fortunate not to have any in Longstone," replied the Mist woman.

Tom Lionhart lunged at Frogley but the other Greytails stopped him. There was a deep rumbling from the Thorns and a hush dropped over the hilltop as everyone focused on the sunset. Laney found the sun too bright to gaze at so she just glanced at it every few seconds. It dropped to halfway, making a fiery semicircle on the western horizon. The singing from the faerie ring grew shriller and Laney thought she could hear someone calling her name.

Around her, those Mists and Greytails still in human form changed to faerie. She closed her eyes for a moment and switched form too. Behind the setting sun rose a pale dot that was hardly visible at first. The sun dipped further until it was just a blazing line of gold. Laney strained her eyes. Was that Saturn behind it? She'd only seen the planet on a poster at school and she knew it would look tiny as it was such a vast distance away. Any humans scanning the horizon might only see it through a telescope but faerie eyes were stronger.

The sun plunged below the skyline and the dot came into focus – a pale-yellow globe circled by its rings of dust and ice. The song from the faerie ring grew more intense, spinning across the hilltop like a whirlpool of noise. Saturn climbed steadily into the sky and then Laney felt it – a rush of power flowing upwards from the ring. It filled her eyes and throat, and made her wings pulse faster.

The power grew in waves and Laney saw that the wings of the nearest Mists were moving faster too. Fletcher, standing beside her, was still in human form. None of the Thorns had switched to faerie form, remaining stiffly in their human bodies. Currents of air swirled around the hilltop and this seemed to increase the tumbling motion of the ring song.

Little by little, the rush of power subsided and Saturn carried on rising. Many of the younger faeries whizzed through the air, pleased with their boost of power. The Greytails chatted and laughed with each other, and began testing out the new strength of their power by summoning creatures. Soon flocks of crows circled the hilltop and foxes gambolled in the field below.

Mr Lionhart held out his arm for a barn owl to perch on.

"Let's leave them to their zoo," Frogley said sneeringly to the other Mists. "We have better things to spend our time on."

With a great flourish, the Mist tribe rose into the air together. They were probably off to do some lake flying, Laney thought bitterly.

"What about her? Isn't she coming?" The fair-haired Mist woman pointed at Laney. "She seems to be a Mist."

"No, she's not a tribe member." Frogley muttered something else and Laney caught the words "bad egg". Frogley tried to fly on, but the Mist woman swept down to Laney.

"Rivers," she said.

"Sorry?" Laney said, surprised.

"You look like a man I used to know, Robert Rivers – are you related?" she said. "You must be."

"He's my dad," said Laney.

"Is he here? And your mother too?" The woman's eyes swept over the Mists. "I don't think he married a Longstone girl. What's your mother's name?"

With the Mist woman's eyes on her, Laney felt she had to answer. "She was Cordelia Brightsea."

"Brightsea? I've never heard of that family. Did she come from somewhere near Longstone?"

Laney flushed, not wanting to admit that she didn't know.

"We should go right away," Frogley murmured to the woman. "We want to make the best of the evening."

With an impatient shrug, the woman flew off with Frogley and the other Mists. Cathy and Leah swooped away without even looking at Laney. Jessie managed to help her mum into the air and they flew off after the others.

The Greytails returned to human form and prowled back down the hillside. Tom rushed ahead as if he was scouting the landscape and looking for prey.

"Can you believe that Mist woman?" hissed Laney to Fletcher. "You don't just come up to someone and demand to know about their family. Fletch?" He was standing stiffly, his arms by his side. "What's up?"

"Nothing. I'm fine." He moved his lips woodenly.

Laney put a hand on his arm. "Hey! Feel those muscles. Have you been working out?" she joked, but he didn't reply. She noticed that none of the other Thorns were moving either.

"What's up with him?" Claudia sprang to Fletcher's side, brimming with energy. She knocked on his forehead. "Come on – don't be an old stick in the mud!"

"Get off me!" said Fletcher stiffly. Then he seemed to wake up a little. "We need to get moving."

Claudia rolled her eyes extravagantly. "Yeah! Sorry if we're slowing you down."

With an effort, Fletcher changed to faerie form. "Straight to the forest then."

Laney took off behind the other two, glancing back at the Edge where the Thorns had begun moving rigidly towards the path that led back to Skellmore. How could they look so stiff and strange after all that energy had poured into them from the faerie ring? It looked as if Saturn Rising hadn't given them any power at all.

CHAPTER
19

They flew west as darkness fell and the moon appeared, crossing the main road that led to Pennington before looping round towards Hobbin Forest. Fletcher plunged down into the trees. Hovering beside a large oak, he started pulling strands of foliage away from the trunk.

"Mistletoe," he said, passing some to Laney.

They each took a bundle of the stringy plant down to the ground. Laney rubbed a scratch on her arm. "These trees grow thicker every time I come here."

"And thornier – look!" Claudia pointed at a cluster of thorns on an oak tree branch.

"Oaks aren't supposed to have thorns on them," said Laney. "Hey, Fletcher?"

But Fletcher had already moved on and they had to hurry to catch up with him. He stopped at last and pointed through the deepening twilight. "Here's the silver birch avenue, where the Avalon project opens. Time to test out the mistletoe – our passport inside!" His eyes gleamed. Laney thought they flashed green for a second, but when she looked again they were grey with gold rings around the pupils, same as usual.

"Are you sure you have enough power?" she said, thinking how stiff and strange the Thorns had appeared after Saturn Rising.

"Yeah, I reckon so." Fletcher walked down the

silver birch avenue.

"Laney!" Claudia clutched her arm. "Look behind you."

Hairy creatures scuffled through the gloomy clearing. "Hobgobbits," said Laney. "Except they're—"

"Bigger, hairier and meaner," finished Claudia.

The creatures turned at the sound of her voice, baring rows of sharp white teeth that glinted through the darkness. Laney and Claudia sprinted down the birch avenue after Fletcher.

"Hobgobbits – coming!" Laney gasped, nearly tripping over her mistletoe.

"They won't bother us here." Fletcher didn't even turn to look at the creatures. His gaze was fixed on the invisible wall ahead. "Are you ready?" He wound the strands of mistletoe around his arms and began walking with his palms facing forwards. His face froze in a look of concentration and a cloudy circle opened in the air. "You go through," he said. "I'll hold it open."

Laney felt around for the edge of the invisible wall, managing to find it and climb through. Claudia leapt through after her. Fletcher followed them, keeping his hand carefully on the gap and as he let his arm fall the cloudy hole disappeared behind them. The Avalon project was just as beautiful at night as it had been in the daytime. The landscape was lit up in silver by the full moon and the pale glow from groups of flying sprites.

"Avalon." Fletcher's face shone. "Home to the Wildwood Arrow."

"Don't go all poetic on us," said Claudia.

Laney gazed around. Privately she thought a bit of poetry fitted the place perfectly. You couldn't even call it countryside. It was nature, pure and simple. Nature as it would have been without people. Meadows of flowers covered gentle curving hills. In the centre rose a towering rocky outcrop crowned with more silver birches. "Does Stingwood want all the Thorns to come and live here?" she asked.

"I don't know." Fletcher's face was calm and still. "But I know I'd live here."

"It's nice," said Claudia, "but it just seems wrong without any animals."

Laney knew what she meant.

Fletcher spread his wings and glided upwards.

"Where are you going?" said Laney.

"To Spine Tree Ridge," he called back, flying towards the rocky outcrop.

The girls soared upwards too and Claudia swooped close, saying into Laney's ear, "We should watch out for Stingwood. I bet he's here somewhere."

As they flew closer to Spine Tree Ridge, Laney could feel the air buzzing with power. "The arrow has to be here, giving out all this energy," she told

Claudia. "And Stingwood must know that."

Claudia looked doubtful. "If he knew he'd found the Myrical, wouldn't he have told the other Thorns?"

Fletcher stopped short in the air and Laney had to throw herself sideways to avoid hitting him. He plunged into the trees growing on the rocky outcrop, flying in and out of them as if he was following a trail.

"I've seen dogs do that," Claudia grinned. "Not while flying, obviously."

"It's here!" Fletcher put his hand on the trunk of a silver birch.

"Really? You mean the arrow's *inside* the tree?" Laney flew down and touched the smooth white bark. "I can't see anything different about it."

"It's well hidden," said Fletcher. "It looks like there was a concealment spell but it's worn away over time. Stingwood must have put magic there to stop other people finding the Myrical."

"Go on then! Grab it." Claudia looked round nervously. "And then we can get out of here."

Fletcher put his palm on the tree and frowned. "I don't know if I can . . . no, wait!" He pulled with his thumb and forefinger, drawing a beautiful arrow with a shining silver tip out of the tree.

"Wow! It's almost like it was meant to be you that got it out," said Laney. "Like in a legend or something – like King Arthur! You know, with the sword in the stone."

"It's not really like King Arthur, because he was a Kestrel faerie," said Claudia.

Laney rolled her eyes. "Yeah, very funny!"

Claudia looked offended. "He was! King Arthur was a Kestrel. Kestrels always fancy themselves as leaders."

Fletcher admired the shape of the arrow. "My dad said in the olden days we used to hunt with arrows like these and that's why they used one to hold the essence of our tribe."

"Can I?" Laney reached for the arrow.

Fletcher frowned. "You can't hold it."

"It's OK. I'll only touch it for a second." Her fingertips brushed along the smooth wood, stopping at the feathers on the fletching. The moonlight dimmed. The trunk of the silver birch turned black and its branches twisted into claws. Laney whipped her hand away and the tree went back to normal. "What was that?" Her heart pounded.

"What was what?" said Fletcher.

"I don't know." Laney stared at the arrow. "It was bad. We should go."

"Fine by me." Claudia fidgeted. "This place is seriously getting on my nerves."

Leaves rustled. A stunted tree close by began to shudder and a deep groan echoed round the ridge.

Laney flew over to the tree. It looked exactly like a twisted tree-man. "Stingwood?" she asked. The greenish-brown trunk held up several misshapen branches. A toothless mouth shape gaped below but there were only creases where the eyes should have been.

Forgetting her fear, Laney pressed one hand to the trunk. "Stingwood, is that you? Can you hear me?"

The tree-man's branches creaked but no more human features appeared.

"He looks terrible!" Claudia drew back. "Urgh! I can't bear to get any closer."

Laney turned to Fletcher. "I think he's stuck like that. Can't we use the Arrow to free him? There must be something we can do."

Fletcher studied the Arrow, not meeting her eyes. "It's his own fault. He must have been trying to keep the Arrow to himself."

The tree moaned and its bark-mouth stretched hideously.

"So this is a spell that backfired on him then?" said Laney.

"Well, he can't have meant to end up looking like that. Seriously!" Claudia shuddered.

"Fletcher! At least try and help him!" cried Laney. "I can't believe you won't do anything for him. Why are you being like this? It's not like you."

"You've never even liked him," said Fletcher.

"I know, but. . ." Laney struggled to explain. It wasn't just that Stingwood was stuck in this hideous tree form. It was that Fletcher didn't seem to care.

Fletcher's eyes flickered, but his hand tightened on the Arrow. "I can't do anything for him anyway. It's too late." And he flew off.

"Maybe when we've locked the Arrow away through the Mencladden Stone he'll go back to normal," said Claudia.

Laney let go of the Stingwood tree. Maybe Claudia was right. Maybe locking the Wildwood Arrow away would allow Stingwood to switch back. They had to go straight to Mencladden Hill and finish this nightmare at sunrise.

Taking to the air, she and Claudia flew after Fletcher. Plants rippled as he passed overhead, drawn to the power of the Arrow. Laney thought that if they could have pulled up their roots and followed, they would.

They found the invisible wall by looking for the discarded mistletoe. Fletcher made the gap in the wall again and climbed through first, not waiting for the others. Laney followed him.

"Hey! Watch it!" Claudia leapt through the fast-closing hole just before it shut completely.

Beyond the wall, darkness lay thickly over the

forest. The moon was hidden behind a cloud and no sprites flew nearby to provide a silvery glow. Laney stumbled down the avenue of silver birches. "Where are you, Fletcher?"

"Slow down a bit, Thorn Boy," grumbled Claudia.

"I'm just here." Fletcher had stopped next to the last birch tree.

A branch scraped against Laney's face. She backed away, straight into another tree. "Ow! Does it seem like the trees are different? I'm sure they're closer together than they were before."

"They're moving." Claudia dropped her voice. "Listen, you can hear them."

A growing creaking and groaning noise came from all around them. Fletcher stood statue-like, holding the arrow. Then without a word he spread his grey wings and soared into the sky.

"Fletcher!" yelled Laney, taking off after him. "You're going the wrong way. The Mencladden Stone is north across the river."

But Fletcher swooped away through the night sky as if he hadn't heard them. The girls flew after him, skimming the treetops.

"He's heading for Skellmore," shouted Claudia.

"Watch out!" Laney pulled Claudia aside as a long tree branch reached up, claw-like, to grab her ankle.

"Freakin' hell!" Claudia climbed higher into the

sky, out of reach of the trees. "What's going on?"

Laney stared down. "I thought being near the Arrow would make the plants and trees act nicer."

A gang of hobgobbits marched between the trees, growling to each other. One caught sight of the girls and spit out a torrent of snarls. The others joined in. Behind them snake-like roots broke out of the earth and slithered across the ground.

"This is dark magic," gasped Claudia. "The forest has gone mad."

Laney stared at the scene below. "It hasn't just gone mad – it's gone everywhere. See – that's where the wood usually stops, at the footpath. Now the trees are growing way past that point. The path's completely overgrown." She pointed to where the path from the lake used to wind along the edge of the wood.

"Unbelievable!" said Claudia. "This must be because of the Arrow."

Laney flew on towards the orange lights of Skellmore and a deep creaking noise split through the darkness. Trees were pressing right up to the fence behind the minimart's back yard.

"We have to make it stop!" snapped Claudia. "If we get the Arrow back and put it through the Mencladden Stone, then everything will go back to normal, right?"

"I hope so," Laney said.

They flew down into the dark minimart yard and changed to human form.

"I bet Fletcher took the Arrow back to his house," said Claudia. "I reckon he wants to show off to all the other Thorns." She dodged round a newly grown prickly hedge.

"Maybe he wants to prove to his dad that he was right," said Laney. "He was really cross when his parents didn't believe that he'd found the Arrow."

The girls ran down the lamplit High Street towards Gnarlwood Lane. Laney caught sight of figures in the park and stopped to peer through the gloom. There were no street lights in the park and it was hard to see. "Wait, Claudia, he's over here!"

"What! Why's he gone to the park?" Claudia said huffily. "He needs to stop mucking around. Seriously!"

Laney had to push thick branches aside to look through the park's metal railings. She could see the towering black shape of the great oak and a small group of figures standing near it. Fletcher was walking stiffly over to them holding the Arrow in both hands. Laney waited for the familiar rush of power from the faerie ring to spread up the oak tree and turn it golden, so that she could see what was going on. But it didn't happen.

Instead, a flash of red lightning arced through the air, hitting the oak's trunk. In that millisecond she saw a tall figure with a hooded black cloak.

Then darkness fell again.

Laney's hands tightened round the railings. "He's here!" she whispered. "I saw the Shadow."

CHAPTER 20

Panic flooded through Laney, making her mind feel slow. She knew she had to do something to get them out of this.

Claudia hissed into her ear. "We have to reach Fletcher before the Shadow does. Laney, are you listening to me? The Shadow could get the Arrow."

Hearing Claudia's voice cut through Laney's panic. "We grab Fletcher and fly him out of here," she said, and she started running, past the railings, the swings and across the football pitch.

Strange stirrings and creakings came from all directions. The full moon came out from behind a cloud, shedding pale, eerie light over the trees and playground. Fletcher was still plodding woodenly towards the oak tree. Several other figures were spread out nearby, standing motionless. Where was the Shadow? For a second she hoped he'd flown away. Then, right next to the oak tree, she saw a place where the darkness was thicker. There was movement inside it, twisting and churning, and she had the feeling she was being watched.

"Laney Rivers." The cold voice came out of the moving darkness. "I have things to show you. Look closer." Writhing shapes formed in the blackness, weaving in and out of each other, forming a sickening pattern that poured into her mind.

She took a step closer and Claudia hissed, "Don't look! It's a dark spell."

With a great effort Laney pulled her gaze away. "Forget it. I'm not falling for your Shadow tricks." She went straight to Fletcher's side. "Fletcher, come back with me! You're not safe here." She was aware of the Shadow listening.

Fletcher stopped his slow shuffle, although he still stared straight ahead. A small bubble of hope rose in Laney and she put her hand on his shoulder, trying hard not to look at the patch of churning darkness. "Fletcher, we have to take the Arrow . . . away." She knew she couldn't mention the Mencladden Stone. "You did the hard bit by finding it. This last part is easy."

Claudia stood at his other side. "Come on, Thorn Boy. We're all fast flyers," she said. "If we make a bolt for it, we can get out of here."

Inside the moving darkness, the Shadow laughed softly.

Fletcher's gold-ringed eyes looked dull, as if a light had disappeared from inside them. He stared ahead, his face unmoving. Laney tightened her grip on his shoulder. "Fletcher?"

His mouth opened. "You . . . must . . ." He struggled for the next word.

"The Shadow will take the Arrow!" Claudia's voice rose. "Get it together – we have to go *right now!*"

"You . . . must . . . leave Skellmore." Fletcher

turned to look at each of them in turn and Laney felt as if his gaze went right through her. "You are . . . not Thorns," he said woodenly. "This place belongs to us." He took another step towards the patch of darkness where the Shadow waited.

"Stop!" Laney sprang in front of him so that he couldn't walk forwards. "It's me, Laney – don't you remember? Think about all the things we're doing – all the things we've done." She searched his face. It was as if a hard shell had formed around the old Fletcher. There had to be a way to break through it. "You're the one that's kept us going all summer. You kept us together – like a team."

The Shadow laughed again and the sound made Laney shudder. "How sweet. Poor Fletcher – always the dependable one."

Fletcher looked down at Laney stiffly. "You are not a Thorn. You must leave."

"Fletcher, please! It's me!" Laney tried to shake him but it was like trying to shake a wall. Then she winced as he pushed her roughly out of his way.

Claudia tried to snatch the Wildwood Arrow but he put up his arm to block her and then resumed his slow shuffling walk towards the Shadow. The motionless figures spread out around the park began walking too.

"They're all Thorns." Claudia peered at their expressionless faces. "He's put a spell on them."

The darkness hissed and the Shadow emerged. His hood hung down, completely concealing his face, while black leather gloves hid his hands. As the folds of his black cloak rippled around him, a stench of decay drifted over to the girls.

"What are you doing to the Thorns?" said Laney. "Let them go!"

"There's no way back for them now." The Shadow's hood moved as he spoke and for a second Laney wondered if she knew his voice. "I wove the perfect core for this spell weeks ago when I found Stingwood with the Arrow. He was trying to use its power to create his little nature project in the forest. He had discovered the Myrical for me and his useless project made the rest easy." With his gloved hand he took hold of one of the oak tree branches and blackness spread along the wood and into the leaves.

Laney's mind whirled. The Shadow had always made plants wither and turn brown. This time the branch was still alive but as black as midnight. "So you knew about the Avalon project," she began. "You knew what Stingwood was doing all along."

"Of course I knew, stupid girl!" the Shadow snarled. "I could have taken the Arrow weeks ago but his project gave me the perfect cover. I added Shadow magic to his pathetic Thorn enchantments and as the power of the Arrow multiplied through the forest, my dark spell spread too." He held up one hand, and Fletcher and all the other Thorns stopped walking. "Root by root and branch by branch; my dark magic has flooded through plants and trees and into the Thorn faeries themselves. Now they are all channels for my power."

"The roots that pinned Craig down in the forest – that was your spell," said Claudia. "And the way the forest's been changing – it was all you!"

The Shadow's hood moved as if he was smiling underneath it. "Don't forget that none of this would have been possible without the Thorns – those tree-hugging, nature-loving fools. And now nature can have its own revenge!" Spreading his gigantic black wings, the Shadow touched the great oak tree and it groaned as if it was in pain. Then a cascade of scraping and creaking began from the surrounding streets.

"Laney," whispered Claudia. "I think the trees are moving again."

The Shadow turned to Fletcher. "Come here, boy."

Fletcher moved forwards woodenly and handed the long arrow with its beautiful shining tip to the Shadow.

"Thank you," said the Shadow silkily. "Now turn around." Fletcher twisted to face Laney and the Shadow raised the Arrow high, spinning it round in the air.

"No!" cried Laney. "Don't hurt him."

The spinning arrow made a grey, smoky vortex that circled down over Fletcher's head. The faerie ring close by sang out a warning, but the vortex spun on, enfolding Fletcher's body in its dark haze. When the whirling air cleared, Fletcher stood before them completely altered. Branches grew where his arms had been. Rough bark covered his face and body, and his legs were welded together into one solid trunk. Yet Laney could tell he was still there underneath.

The Shadow laughed. "He makes a good tree." His voice dropped menacingly. "And if you try to release him from my spell he will die. They'll all die. Their life force is connected to the Arrow and the Arrow is mine."

"I don't believe you!" Laney's eyes pricked with tears and she reached out to Fletcher. "Listen to me, Fletcher. Just hold on and we'll find a way to free you."

"Take them to their houses and lock them in," commanded the Shadow. "Make sure they don't escape."

The other Thorns advanced silently on the girls, their faces blank. Grey-haired Mr Willowby was there, and Mr and Mrs Thornbeam, who walked right past Fletcher without a second look. Laney tried to fly but Mr Willowby got hold of her and pulled her arms behind her back. Claudia got halfway into the air before Mrs Thornbeam grabbed her ankles and pulled her down again.

"You're a coward!" Laney shouted at the Shadow.

He clenched one fist and red lightning sparked in his hand. "I will ignore that for now," he said, "because I know someone who has a plan for you, Laney Rivers, and he has Many Eyes."

Laney shivered, not knowing what he meant.

A handful of forlorn crows flew over their heads. "Crows!" Claudia yelled. "Bring the Greytails!" But the crows sped away from Skellmore.

Laney's middle finger prickled and heat rushed through her hands. She used the heat, pushing Mr Willowby hard and making him fall over.

"Do you know what happens when a tree gets struck by lightning, Laney Rivers?" The Shadow towered over Fletcher, rolling a ball of red lightning in one hand. "Would you like to see?"

Behind the rough bark, Laney could see Fletcher's face but it looked as though his eyes were closed. She thought of how steady and calm he'd been all summer and her arms dropped to her sides. She couldn't bear losing him.

The red lightning crackled in the Shadow's hand. "It's good that you've seen sense. Take them back to their houses for now."

Laney didn't resist when Mr Willowby grabbed

her arms again and pulled her away. At the park gate she twisted round and saw the Shadow slip the Wildwood Arrow under his cloak before sinking back into the darkness. Fletcher stood alone, his branches frozen into position.

The streetlamp next to the minimart flickered and Laney's stomach filled with cold dread. This wasn't the High Street she knew. Brambles clambered over the walls and rooftops of the shops and houses. A hedge bursting with sharp spines blocked the road at both ends and it was climbing higher with every moment. The ground trembled beneath their feet and wiry black roots burst through the concrete and snaked across the pavement.

"Where are the humans?" Claudia dodged one root with a shudder. "Why aren't they out here screaming about all of this?"

Laney peered into the dark minimart window and saw Mrs Mottle lying on the floor. She noticed the woman's arm twitching even though her eyes stayed closed. "Claudia, look at Craig's mum. She looks as if she's sleeping." Suddenly Laney caught a strong scent and recognised it straight away. "I can smell the valerian again, just like at Gwen's house." She peered at Mrs Mottle's sleeping form. "Maybe humans are more easily affected by it than faeries."

The scent grew stronger and Laney tried not to breathe in too deeply. Mr Willowby gave her a push, making her lurch forwards. She caught sight of people slumped in the chairs of the hairdresser's salon and others lying on the floor with scissors and combs in their hands. "They're asleep in the hairdressers too. They must have been like this for hours. It must have happened while we were at Saturn Rising."

Claudia stared at the wall of the pet shop in horror. "Oh no! I can't believe they did that." The two gigantic cat's eyes were held shut by rope-like stems covered in sharp thorns. The wall let out a long wail as the stems closed tighter. "You can't do this!" Claudia struggled against her captors. "You can't enslave the Greytails!"

"Claudia!" hissed Laney. "Don't lose it, OK? We'll get out of this."

The Thorns dragged Laney and Claudia silently up Beacon Way. Halfway up, Claudia broke free and raced into The Cattery. Mrs Thornbeam tried to recapture her but the Cattery houses spat and snarled when she came too close. A gang of cats formed a barricade across the road, hissing at the Thorns. Dizzy sprang on to Claudia's shoulder, meowing shrilly, her black fur on end.

"Claudia! Where've you been?" Tom flew down the road. "Get in here quickly! You've no idea what's going on."

"What? You mean about the Thorns turning

evil?" Claudia stamped on a bramble that had slid past the line of cats.

"Well – yeah!" Tom scowled. "So you do know then."

Laney lunged sideways to get away from the Thorns and cross the line into The Cattery, but Mr Willowby pulled her back with surprising strength. "I can't get away," she yelled to Claudia.

"I'll come and find you, OK?" Claudia shouted. "They won't be able to stop me."

The Thorns pushed Laney up to Oldwing Rise, past several people who were sleeping on the path or the road. Laney swallowed. They must have fallen asleep exactly where they stood when they first breathed in the valerian. Craig was snoring gently on the path with vines crawling across him. Laney's unease grew as she passed each sleeper. There was no one to protect them. She had to find a way to break the Shadow's power over the Thorns, especially Fletcher, but there was no point going back for him until the other Thorns were out of the way.

As she was shoved along Oldwing Rise in the gloom, she saw that her own house had been imprisoned in brambles too. Her dad's face was peering out through a small gap in the leaves and vines that covered the upstairs window. The way in was barred by thick wooden stems that had wound sinuously across the wall and over the front door.

At the end of the lane, another spiky thicket blocked the footpath out of the village.

"Laney!" her dad called faintly, and the door juddered as he tried to force it open.

Blank-faced, Mr Willowby dragged Laney to her front door. He touched the vines and they parted instantly. The front door burst open and Mr Rivers stood there brandishing a large pipe wrench. "Quick – get in!" he said. "Stay back, Willowby. I don't want to have to use this on a man of your age."

Laney stumbled inside and Mr Rivers slammed the door shut behind her. With a soft scraping noise the vines grew back, covering the square of glass at the top of the door in seconds and cutting out the orange light from the street lamp.

Mr Rivers hurried to the sitting-room window, which was also covered in vines, and peered through the stems. "He's gone," he said finally. "Laney, where've you been? I wanted to come out and look for you but I couldn't leave Kim and Toby."

Laney drew a shaky breath. "Dad. Something's happened to Fletcher."

CHAPTER 21

Laney suddenly realised that she was still in faerie form. She closed her eyes and changed back. With everything else that had happened she'd forgotten about hiding her faerie form from Toby and Kim.

"You don't have to worry about anyone seeing you," said her dad. "Kim and Toby can't look at anything right now." He drew back to give Laney a view of the sitting room.

Kim and Toby lay sleeping on the sofa. Toby stirred, resting his cheek on his chubby little hand.

"How long have they been like this?" said Laney. "There's the scent of valerian on the High Street and along Beacon Way. Did that send them to sleep?"

"Yes, there's valerian everywhere," explained her dad. "Just enough to send all humans into an enchanted sleep. It was released just before the plants grew out of control. The Thorns have been flying past every ten minutes, releasing more to keep up the concentration in the air." He looked through the window, peering at the sky. "You can't see the spell in the dark, but when the sun shines you'll see little bits of it floating like green dust."

Laney knelt down next to Toby. He looked so tiny – too little to be caught up in all of this.

"They'll be OK as long as they don't sleep for too long," said her dad. "Staying in an enchanted sleep for more than a day could cause memory loss when they wake up."

Laney stood up, her hands growing hot. She shoved them in her pockets. "We have to fly them out of here. Then I'll come back for Fletcher."

Her dad looked at her, amazed. "Laney, you're twelve years old. I don't expect you to do all that. Anyway I've already tried to fly away with Toby but the Thorns chased me and I couldn't risk a fight where he might get hurt."

"It's not the Thorn's fault. They're being controlled." Laney remembered that her dad knew nothing of the Wildwood Arrow and the Shadow. She wished she'd told him more before now.

"There's something you're not telling me." He frowned as if he'd read her mind. "You said something had happened to Fletcher. What is it? What's going on?"

Laney took a deep breath and told her father everything – from the Shadow faerie and the Crystal Mirror to what had happened earlier that evening.

"What?" her dad exploded. "There's no Shadow faerie living here – the last one was seen years ago, before you were even born. Who's filled your head with this rubbish?"

"It's not rubbish, dad! The Shadow is real – I've seen him. He's been searching for the Myricals and now he's got the Wildwood Arrow."

"Laney! The Myricals were lost *years* ago.

Countless Elders have looked for them but no one's ever been able to find them."

"The Shadow's got one right now! He's taken the Arrow and he's done something to it – infected it with dark magic – and he's using it to control the Thorns. He turned Fletcher into a tree and now Fletcher can't move or speak or anything!" Laney took a deep breath. "I'm going back there to help him."

"You must be joking! You are *not* going back out there!" Mr Rivers said firmly. "Fletcher will be all right. The Thorns will look after their own, but it's too dangerous for you and I won't allow it."

"He won't be all right. He looked awful!" cried Laney. "What if it hurts being stuck in that tree shape?"

Kim turned restlessly on the sofa and muttered something in her sleep. Laney lowered her voice, saying urgently. "We can't just stay here and do nothing."

"We have to protect ourselves and wait it out. Some of the Mists got out just before the plants closed in. I saw them flying away. They'll go over to Gillforth and tell Frogley and the others, and then help will come. Once more faeries get here we can defeat the Thorns together. The humans are safe for now. We can make ourselves even safer. I know a good spell – I learned it growing up. It's a Water

Binding enchantment and if I weave it all round the house it will keep the Thorns out. My dad taught it to me."

"What if Frogley doesn't send help?" said Laney. "What if the Thorns make the valerian stronger and we fall asleep like the humans?"

"Listen, I don't have time to argue. I have to go and start the protection spell, OK? Stay calm for me and look after Kim and Toby."

Laney thought quickly. She had to help Fletcher, and once her dad's protection spell was done she would be trapped inside the house. That meant she had to leave now.

"Stay back, Laney." Mr Rivers wrenched at the front door, only managing to open it a tiny crack. He yanked at the branches barring the gap, snapping them off and throwing them to the ground.

Immediately more branches grew in their place – thicker, stronger branches covered in thorns. Vines pulled at the door, banging it shut. Mr Rivers screwed up his face as he forced it open again and dragged the branches apart. Thorns scraped his skin as he climbed through the hole he'd made, leaving long red gashes down his arms. Laney climbed through after him, wincing as a spike stuck into her neck.

Mr Rivers waded through the front garden, his face set with determination. "I thought I told you to stay inside! Now, keep back. I haven't used this Longstone spell for years, so it could take me a couple of tries."

At the word *Longstone*, a picture of the Mist visitors she'd seen at Skellmore Edge jumped into Laney's mind. "There were two Mists from Longstone at the Saturn Rising. One of them knew you."

Mr Rivers wiped his hands on his jeans. "Gotta concentrate on this, Laney."

"Dad?" She couldn't stop herself. "Where did you meet Mum? Where did she live before you got married? You've never told me."

"Laney! This isn't the time. Save it for later." The air trembled and her dad transformed, dark-blue wings unfolding from his back.

Laney stared in amazement. She'd never seen him in faerie form before. He looked younger – full of energy. He pointed in the air and a fine curtain of rain fell steadily, separating the house from the lane like a sheet of grey glass. Laney noticed the sky growing lighter in the east. The sun would rise soon. She had to leave now before her dad finished this spell.

Wings rustled overhead. Laney looked up, expecting to see the Thorns taking valerian around the village. A black-winged figure burst through the curtain of water, freezing it then shattering it instantly. Shards of ice flew in all directions, striking Laney's skin like vicious needles.

Mr Rivers fell backwards. The Shadow landed in front of him and folded his great black wings. "You didn't answer her question, Robert. Where did her mother come from? Why won't you tell her?"

"Laney, get back inside!" Mr Rivers got up and faced the Shadow. "How do you know my name? What do you want?"

"Forget the binding spell, Robert. You know you don't do that kind of magic any more," the Shadow said coldly. "I cannot allow you to complete it. This place is now under my control."

"This is my home and no one else will come near it." Mr Rivers rose into the air, conjuring the sheet of water again. "Especially not someone who uses a dead faerie's dust to help themselves to power. You disgust me!"

"Dad – don't!" Laney saw the red lightning crackle in the Shadow's hand.

"You should listen to her, Robert," said the Shadow silkily. "She's felt my lightning strike before."

Laney's dad clenched his fists and blue lightning sizzled inside them. Flinging his arms out he threw a stream of pale lightning bolts at the Shadow, who countered it with a barrage of red. Mr Rivers' lightning held back the Shadow's at first, but gradually the stream of blue began to weaken. With a sudden flick of his hand, the Shadow aimed a bolt at Laney and her dad dived to block it. The bolt hit him in the stomach and he collapsed, hitting his head on the concrete path.

Laney ran to him. His body changed back to human form and he lay still, eyes closed. A cold fear crept around her heart. "Dad, get up!"

"He should not have got in my way and neither should you," said the Shadow, spreading his bat-like wings. "I *will* have all the Myricals. Your efforts to imprison the Crystal Mirror will not delay me for ever." He soared upwards into the air.

Laney took hold of her dad's arms and pulled him up the path and through the front door, tearing at the vines as they got in her way. She managed to drag him inside. Then she knelt by him, studying his face. She was sure he was breathing. She took his pulse, reassured by the steady beat.

"Dad?" There was no response. "Dad, can you hear me?" Her heart ached. He should never have tried to fight the Shadow, especially as he was so out of practice with magic.

She leaned back against the wall, her hand over her eyes. Her dad had just wanted to protect her and that's what had got him hurt. One by one it felt as if all the people close to her were being taken away.

CHAPTER 22

When her heart stopped pounding, Laney fetched a pillow and eased it underneath her dad's head. His eyes flickered and he groaned softly. She leaned closer. "Dad, are you OK?"

"Just . . . tired," he murmured. "I'm sorry I . . . didn't believe you about the Shadow." He closed his eyes again.

Wanting to be near him, she got a pillow for herself and lay down close by.

When she opened her eyes again, tiny patches of sunlight were glinting through the dark, plant-infested windows. She must have fallen asleep. How could she have wasted time like that? She checked her dad's pulse again. It was still quite steady. "Dad?" She shook his shoulder gently and he muttered something but didn't open his eyes. A large lump had swollen on his forehead. She knew he needed a doctor.

She passed the sitting room where Kim and Toby slept on and went to her bedroom, where she managed to open a window very slightly. Grabbing a pair of scissors she hacked away at the vines and leaves that blocked the glass. Before the plants grew back, Laney looked out across a deserted Skellmore in the pale morning light. Valerian, with its tall stems and little white flowers, rippled gently in every garden. Brambles covered the roads and the church was hidden under a mass of clinging vines that had climbed to the top of the steeple. Trees stood in parts of the graveyard where they'd never been before and roots poked from cracks in the earth. The sun rose over the rooftops, revealing a million tiny green flecks floating in the air like dust. The valerian spell.

She had to escape and find Claudia quickly. She needed her Mist magic to work for once. She would need every tiny bit of power she had.

Branches covered with jagged thorns grew across the gap she'd made, barring the way. She took hold of the nearest stem, remembering how she'd defeated the roots that had imprisoned Craig in the forest. The thorns dug into her hand and a drop of blood ran down her skin. Ignoring the pain, she held tight and felt her hands grow hot. The branch shuddered and went limp, black marks were imprinted on the stem where her fingers had been.

Forcing the window open wider, Laney climbed halfway out. She grabbed hold of any branches in her way. A thick yellow vine wound itself tightly round her throat. Panicking, she tried to pull it loose, her fingers burning with heat. The vine darkened where she'd touched it, then it unwound and slithered away. With little time to think, Laney climbed the rest of the way out then stretched her wings and flew.

Circling over the rooftops she took one last look

at her home, now lost under a tangle of branches. Her family were lying helpless in there. It was hard to fly away from them but the only way to fix this was to get the Arrow.

She swooped low across Beacon Way, and as she got closer to The Cattery she heard a fierce yowling. Thorns were standing at the entrance to the road, led by Fletcher's dad, Mr Thornbeam. His skin was a brownish-green and leaves sprouted from his arms. There was no expression in his normally kind eyes. The bungalow on the corner growled at the Thorns, its sharp spines standing on end.

"Laney – watch out!" called Claudia.

Tom and Charlie Springer flew past, their eyes fixed on the line of guarding Thorns.

"Now!" Tom directed a volley of lightning at the Thorns. Then he flew back and a pack of cats streamed past him, making for gaps in the Thorns' defences.

Charlie swooped down, this time brandishing a large pair of shears. He sliced wildly at the Thorns, sending leaves and twigs flying until Mr Thornbeam wrenched them from his hands.

"Here!" Tom tossed Charlie a pair of pruners and Charlie dived in to attack again.

Laney saw her chance, weaving round the fighting and landing in The Cattery.

"Over here!" Claudia took her to the shelter of

the Lionhart house with its animal-patterned walls and its warning written above the door: *Do not provoke the beast within.*

"We've been keeping the Thorns out of our road all night," said Claudia. "Only a few of them seem to be able to transform and use their wings, which makes it easier. A few Greytails left the village but we decided to stay and fight. My mum's making a spell to counter the valerian because we reckon it's getting stronger and stronger."

"Did you tell them about the Arrow?"

"Keep your voice down!" Claudia said urgently. "No, and I don't want to! I know Tom would go after it – he thinks he's a Greytail hero or something. Then the Shadow would catch him and kill him."

"We can't fix this without getting back the Arrow." Laney's eyes clouded over. "My dad's hurt – he needs a doctor. We're running out of time!"

"Have you got a plan?"

"We need Fletcher. But we need stuff from Gwen's house first."

"Great." Claudia sighed. "I just hope the dark spell that chased us out isn't waiting."

Dizzy came round the corner and sat down on her haunches, gazing accusingly at Laney. "Dizzy, I'm going with Laney to sort this mess out," said Claudia. "Cover for me, all right?"

Dizzy blinked slowly and uttered a low yowl.

Claudia's face was pale. "I'm ready, Water Girl. Let's get out of here before we change our minds."

Laney spread her wings. She knew nothing would change hers.

They circled over fields to reach Gnarlwood Lane without going too close to the park or the High Street. A huge fallen tree lay across the main road out of the village.

"That's clever," Claudia said grimly, looking at the blocked road. "Now the humans can't get into the village."

"And they can't get out either," said Laney.

They glided down to Gnarlwood Lane and hurried to Gwen's front gate. A bramble caught at Claudia's ankles and scratched her skin. "Stupid Thorns and their plants!" she cursed, kicking the bramble away.

"It's not the Thorns' fault," Laney said quickly. She thought of Fletcher, his arms trapped into their branch form, and a lump came to her throat.

"It's definitely Stingwood's fault! He planned that Avalon place just for his own tribe and he messed around with the Arrow's power to do it," Claudia fired up. "None of the other Thorns stopped him either."

"They didn't know this would happen," said Laney.

Claudia fixed her cat-like eyes on Laney. "What if the Shadow was telling the truth when he said it was too late to change the Thorns back?"

"That *thing* wouldn't know how to tell the truth. I don't believe a word he says." Laney scanned the house, wondering if anything was waiting behind the dark windows.

Claudia pushed on the gate. "Well, there's only one way to find out if it's safe in there."

They rushed through the long-stemmed valerian to Gwen's door where Claudia fiddled with the lock until it clicked open. The door swung wide. Gwen's sitting room looked the same as ever with no sign of shadowy movement in the corners. Claudia sprang inside and checked under the coffee table and behind the sofa. "All clear!"

A snarling came from the bottom of the lane and Laney shut the door fast. "There's a gang of hobgobbits coming this way but I don't think they saw me."

Claudia went to the window. "Not just any hobgobbits either. These are twice as big as usual and probably twice as hairy. They are creatures of the forest so the Shadow magic in the Arrow must be affecting them too."

Laney paused by the passageway that led to Gwen's plant house. "I can't hear anything." They looked at each other and crept down the corridor.

"Gwen's not here." Laney scanned the empty plant house. "No sign of that shadowy spell either."

Claudia tilted her head for a moment. "She's not in the house at all. There's no sound or smell of her, and the valerian scent is weaker than it was before."

"Do you think she broke the enchantment?" said Laney eagerly.

"If she did, then why isn't she here helping us?"

"Maybe she left another note." Laney ran to the kitchen but there was nothing.

"Face it: we're on our own." Claudia drummed her fingers on the worktop. "So what now?"

Laney took a deep breath. "The Thorns draw their power from plants and herbs. So we need to find the right one to release Fletcher from the Shadow's grip."

Claudia raised her eyebrows. "Herbs! That's your plan? We're fighting the most evil faerie power that exists and you want to use *herbs*."

Laney flushed. She looked inside Gwen's cupboard and examined the jars and bottles on the worktop. "Here is it!" She seized the padlocked jar she'd looked at before. "Remember Gwen said that this was the strongest thing she had."

"It's just dried ferns!" Claudia folded her arms. "This is a waste of time."

"No, I remember her saying that they were usually harmless, but these ones were mega strong."

Laney read the tiny label on the jar. "*Moonwort from my plant house: picked on July 15th.* That's my birthday."

Claudia looked at the label. "It was picked this year too. Hey, do you think that means. . ."

"Yeah. That's why it's special." Laney stared at the delicate dry leaves inside the jar. "She picked it on the night of the red moon – the night I Awakened." She swallowed. It seemed like everything came back to this. Why *had* she Awakened at the red moon? Had she been cursed by gaining her powers on that unlucky night? Not even the Spirit Smoke had been able to answer her questions – exploding as soon as she'd asked to see what had happened.

She pressed her lips tight. If the red moon had given the moonwort plant its special strength, then fine. As long as she could use it to get Fletcher back she didn't care.

"We can put a few of the leaves into some elixir." She opened the fridge and took out three bottles of green elixir. Then she poured them all into a big empty lemonade bottle from Gwen's recycling box.

Claudia struggled with the padlock on the jar. "Where's the key for this? I can't open it."

"There isn't time for that." Laney grabbed the jar and threw it on the floor, smashing it into dozens of pieces.

"Laney!" gasped Claudia.

Laney picked up the moonwort, dropped some of the leaves into the lemonade bottle and shook it. "The Shadow's taken over the village. Fletcher's been turned into a tree and your family are fighting to keep the Thorns out of The Cattery. Are you really going to worry about a smashed jar?"

"I guess not." Claudia eyed her doubtfully. "But you're not the same girl you were a few weeks ago, Laney Rivers."

CHAPTER 23

Laney and Claudia hid behind a wall near the park, carrying the lemonade bottle with its elixir and moonwort leaves.

"We should test this stuff before we use it," whispered Claudia. "We need to know what it does."

Laney spotted a black root that had burst through the pavement and was slithering towards them. She poured a single drop of mixture on to the root and they watched it transform, gradually turning back to brown and burying itself in the earth again.

Laney and Claudia exchanged looks. "This could actually work." Claudia's eyes gleamed. "I'm just worried that when we break cover to give this to Fletcher, the Shadow will see us. And even if Fletcher changes back there'll still be only three of us to fight him."

"Maybe if we're fast enough we can cure a few Thorns before he reaches us."

Claudia shook her head. "We need a way to spread this stuff so that all the Thorns get cured at the same time. If you can make it rain over the park, then I can throw the elixir into the cloud where it'll mix with the rain and pour on everyone at once."

"What if I can't make it rain?" hissed Laney. "Or if the rain comes out *wrong*?"

"Maybe it would be easier with two of you." Claudia jerked her head towards a slim figure that had just darted into the doorway of the hairdresser's.

"Jessie? You're kidding me! She'd never help."

"You have to try," said Claudia. "You're both Mists and she's been using water magic for longer."

"Yeah, I bet she'll mention that a couple of times. OK, here goes." Laney ran quickly over to Jessie, dodging around the trees and brambles that had forced their way through the tarmac.

"What do you want?" Jessie shrank back into the doorway. "Go away – the Thorns will hear you and come looking for us."

Laney forced herself to say it. "I need your help with a Mist spell."

"No way! I'm not staying here; I'm flying north to find my dad. My mum can't get out of here by herself – she's not strong enough. I'm going to make him come back and help us." She glared at Laney. "Stop playing the hero and go back to your family."

"My dad's injured, and Toby and my stepmum have been sent to sleep by the valerian," Laney told her. "If we can free the Thorns from the Shadow's spell—"

"Oh, not this again! When will you learn? There IS NO Shadow."

Laney made a huge effort to stay calm. "I don't have time to argue with you about it. I need to make a rain shower big enough to give all the Thorns a dose of this. I'm going to mix it in with the rain."

She showed Jessie the lemonade bottle. "Now, are you going to help me or not?"

"I'm not," Jessie snapped. "Unless . . . is that Gwen's elixir?"

"Why?" Laney looked at her warily.

"I need some for my mum, you idiot! To restore her strength."

"Help me make it rain and I'll get the elixir for you." She pulled the bottle back as Jessie made a grab for it. "You can't have this. There's something extra in it and it's really strong."

"Fine then." Jessie looked sulky. "Let's do this stupid rain shower. But if the Thorns catch you, I'm not coming to help you."

"Imagine my surprise," said Laney. "We need to make it rain above the park first, then spread the shower to cover all of Skellmore. If we fly high there's less chance we'll be seen."

Signalling to Claudia to join them, Laney ran round the corner into the back yard of the minimart followed by Jessie. "You just need to keep an eye on things while we summon the rain," Laney told Claudia. "Let us know if anyone's coming."

"Have you got her believing in this Shadow rubbish too?" asked Jessie incredulously. "You're all deluded."

"Trust me: you'll soon see for yourself, whether you want to or not." Claudia spread her wings.

"Let's do this."

They soared high over Skellmore. A blanket of grey cloud had drifted in, turning the air cold, but there was no sign of any rain. Below them, the Thorns patrolled the streets while gangs of hobgobbits practised random destruction, knocking over bins and tearing posters off the shop walls.

Laney's heart jumped when she saw the still shape near the great oak tree. Fletcher. She flew on, fighting the urge to go over to him. Words couldn't help him now. He needed her to break the poisonous hold the Shadow had over the Arrow.

Several other statue-like forms were dotted around the park. Laney wondered if they were Thorns who had tried to break free or whether the Shadow had just transfixed them for fun. On the far side of Skellmore a group of Thorns flew low over the rooftops and the green specks of the valerian spell glinted in the air behind them.

The Shadow was nowhere to be seen.

"This is high enough." Jessie hovered, her curly hair tangling in the wind. "We need to bring the cloud closer before we release the water. It's too far away right now. Just pull it down with your mind, a little bit at a time. And try not to muck it up."

Laney passed Claudia the lemonade bottle, ignoring the sting in Jessie's words. Then she raised her arms to the sky, copying the other Mist girl closely. Patches of cloud broke away from the grey cloudbank and drifted down. Laney stretched higher, wishing everything would speed up. She knew the clouds were way above and it took time for them to float down, but every second increased the chance that someone might look up and see them.

"Come on," she muttered under her breath.

"You're hopeless, aren't you?" said Jessie. "Your arms are too spiky. Just hold them slightly curved and then move your hands in a rhythm, like you're an ocean."

Claudia raised one eyebrow. "Yeah, come on, Laney. Be like an ocean."

Laney tried to copy Jessie's hand movements, but she felt like she was doing it all wrong. Streaks of cloud vapour rushed at her, wrapping their cold, clammy arms around her skin.

Jessie scowled at Laney's efforts as she summoned several round puffs of perfect cloud and collected them above her head.

A high yowl made the hairs rise on Laney's arms. Claudia thrust the lemonade bottle into her hands, her face drawn with worry. "I'm going to check on everyone in The Cattery. I think the Thorns may have broken through." She raced away, wings at full stretch.

Laney looked down at the crescent shape of

The Cattery. There was a loud bang and figures running.

Jessie pulled her bundle of cloud nearer so that it floated just above her fingertips. "We're ready," she said, then added fiercely, "but don't forget – we're getting the elixir for my mum as soon as we've done this."

"I know! I said so, didn't I? How do we make the cloud release the rain?"

"Just tell it to – and mean it." Jessie took the lemonade bottle. "You'd better let me do this. Once the rain has begun I'll scatter it so that it mixes in."

Laney's wings fluttered faster. This was it. It was time. "After three then? One, two, three. . ." She stared at the cloud above her head. "Rain!"

A water drop hit her face, then another and another.

"Rain!" Laney called more loudly.

"Control it!" said Jessie. "Don't let it go wild. We want a steady flow not just a burst of rain that's over in a few seconds."

Laney looked over at Jessie. The other girl was bringing down sheets of raindrops in an even pattern. She closed her eyes and tried harder. *Rain. Let it rain.* Her hands grew hotter and the burn mark on her middle finger throbbed painfully.

"No! What are you doing?" screamed Jessie.

"What?" Laney opened her eyes.

Jessie was staring at Laney's hands in horror. "You freak! You absolute freak."

A flicker of orange leapt in the palms of Laney's hands. Raindrops fell on to her skin and sizzled. "I'm not doing anything. It's not me," she said desperately. "I just told it to rain."

"I knew this would happen." Jessie's low voice was vehement. Her eyes narrowed. "You can't even make it rain properly and it's one of the easiest Mist skills there is. You've never been one of us. You may have burst the water pipes at school on the day you Awakened but that doesn't make you a true Mist. I've always known from the start that you weren't normal."

"What do you mean?" Laney's hands glowed hotter than ever and the glimmer of orange leapt in them again.

"Don't you remember the sand and water table at nursery school?" Jessie glared at her. "We were playing there together and we went for the same toy and then you boiled the water."

An image flashed through Laney's head of a small Jessie crying and clutching her hands. "I scalded you. But I wasn't even Awake then."

"You've *never* been a Mist. There's something wrong with you." Jessie's face twisted in disgust. "I'll get the elixir myself. I don't want your help to find it anyway." She thrust the lemonade bottle back into

Laney's arms and, with a blast of rain, flew away.

"I *am* a Mist. I'm just still learning what to do," Laney called after her. She looked down at her hands. The tiny glint of orange had vanished. She didn't understand – where had it come from?

Claudia came back from The Cattery, circling to avoid the falling rain. "My mum's made a shell shield and it's holding the Thorns off for now." She stared at Jessie flying away. "What's wrong with her?"

Laney shrugged, fumbling with the top of the bottle. She should have known Jessie would leave her without finishing the job. But the Thorns had to be freed and the Arrow recaptured. She would throw the elixir and moonwort mixture into the cloud herself. It would work. It just had to.

From the corner of her eye she saw a dark shape. The bottle lid wouldn't twist. She tried to wrench it but it was stuck. At the edge of her sight, the dark shape grew larger.

Then Claudia screamed.

CHAPTER
24

The Shadow's cloak streamed outwards and his wings pulsed like a black heartbeat. Laney was hypnotised for a moment. Then she tore the lid off the bottle and shook it frantically. The green potion arced through the air, splitting into hundreds of little drops and merging into the cloud vapour. Laney's heart sank as she saw the rain starting to fade and a band of sunshine sweep over the High Street. The bottle was nearly empty. Had she done enough to help the Thorns?

"Laney!"

Claudia's shout forced her into action and she dodged away from the Shadow, who swung round to grab at her. She folded in her wings and let herself fall head first. The air pushed back at her but she held her course, heading for one small figure that stood immobile in the park. The growing darkness told her that the Shadow was following.

She slowed down too late and hit the ground hard, but she managed to get up and run, her legs almost giving way beneath her. The sight of Fletcher gave her extra strength and she clutched the last of the bottled potion to her side.

A glint of sunshine from the edge of the clouds made the rainwater glisten on the grass. The rain had at least covered the park but dark roots and brambles still lay across the football pitch. Was the moonwort leaf working?

With a crash the Shadow landed, splitting a hole in the earth and making the ground tremble. "How dare you!" his voice shook. "I should kill you for this and I would love to do it." He clenched one gloved hand. "But *he* would not like that. So, Laney Rivers, how much pain do you think I can make you feel without letting you die?"

Laney's eyes flicked sideways. The Shadow stood between her and Fletcher.

He caught her look. "Ah, yes! *Perhaps* it would be more fun if we let Fletcher feel the pain for you."

Laney caught a flash of movement from above and a large metal TV aerial landed on the Shadow, knocking him to the ground.

"*Perhaps* it would be more fun if we dropped stuff on your head," said Claudia, brushing her hands together. "Ow! That was freakin' heavy!"

Laney raced to Fletcher, whose body was now more tree-like than ever. His skin was rough and furrowed, and for a second she wondered whether the changes had gone too far.

"Fletcher?" She studied what had been his face. "Can you hear me? You have to try and wake up." She poured the last drips of the elixir moonwort mixture where she thought his mouth should be and it trickled slowly down the trunk. Two deep creases above the mouth shape should have been his eyes, but they didn't open.

The Shadow rose with a howl of fury and let loose a great stream of red lightning at Claudia, who slumped to the ground. Then he rounded on Laney.

Laney hesitated. She didn't want to leave Fletcher, but what about Claudia?

"Urrrrm. . ." came a deep groan. Not from the Shadow this time, but from the tree behind her. The Fletcher tree. She caught her breath.

His nose and mouth emerged from the bumps and knots of the tree trunk. The bark thinned, warming in colour, and his eyes opened.

"Fletcher!" Laney grinned. "It worked!" His eyes were gold-ringed with grey underneath, same as always.

"What was in that?" The Shadow seized the empty lemonade bottle. "Tell me, girl."

Laney thought of the label on the moonwort jar and the fern-like leaves picked on the night of the red moon – the night she'd Awakened. "It's something strong." She tried to hold her voice steady. "And I bet the other Thorns are waking too because I threw most of it into the rain." Behind the Shadow's cloak, she saw Claudia get up and limp away. She hoped Claudia was going to get help – though there might be no one left who could help them.

The Shadow stepped closer. "Cursed child! You were cursed from the moment you were born, right from the moment you brought your diseased magic into our world." He worked up a ball of lightning between his hands. "But I am not allowed to let you die. However, I *can* kill your Thorn friend instead. The Thorns are a stupid tribe, after all."

"Laney," croaked Fletcher. "Get out of here."

"Hurry up, Fletch!" Laney held one of his branch-arms. He was changing too slowly.

The lightning ball crackled red in the Shadow's hands. Laney put herself between the Shadow and Fletcher. "Why can't you just take the Wildwood Arrow and go?" she yelled, and her hands grew so hot she had to clasp them together.

"There is so much more the Arrow could do here," said the Shadow. "A tree root has great power – over time it can topple buildings and break the ground apart. The Thorns' plan, to create a place without humans, was a good start but it takes Shadow magic to truly wipe the human vermin from our land. That is a worthy use of a Myrical." The dark hood hanging over his face moved and the rotting smell from his cloak began to make Laney feel dizzy.

"So that's your plan: to get rid of the humans?" Laney said as she felt Fletcher's branch-arm turn to skin under her hand. If she could keep the Shadow talking there would be time for Fletcher to change completely. "Is that what you're using the Arrow for?"

"No more words." The Shadow's gloved hand fastened painfully over her wrist and he dragged her away from Fletcher. "Out of my way, unless you want to feel my rage." He let go of her, sending her crashing to the ground.

"No!" Laney scrambled up. "Don't touch him. You've already hurt my dad." She gripped the back of the Shadow's black cloak and pulled in desperation. The material began to smoke under her fingers. There was a flicker of orange and a tiny hole with ragged edges appeared in the cloak.

Laney fell back, her heart juddering unevenly. Her hands were blazing with heat and, giving into instinct, she grabbed hold of the Shadow's cloak again. Pain shot through her hands into her fingers and the burn mark on her middle finger became a white-hot point of agony.

The Shadow yelled and thrust Laney away from him. Tiny flames burned where she'd touched him, licking along the material. Hastily he clamped his hands over his cloak to put them out.

Laney breathed in sharply. Lifting her hands, she studied the fire burning in the centre of her palms. The flames were edged with orange and had a pure gold centre. There was no pain in her hands any more, just a deep sense of warmth. The pent-up feeling she'd had for weeks – the feeling that something was trapped inside her – was gone completely. Breathing fast, she watched the fire burn higher, climbing as her spirits rose.

"Impossible!" the Shadow hissed. "That is a hoax! You've got some Elder to bewitch you. Your friend shall pay the price – in pain."

Laney rushed at him, pressing the flames on to him and burning another hole in his cloak. She reached for his hood, singeing the edges of the black material. The Shadow grabbed her throat, unfolding his vast leathery wings and lifting her off the ground. Ice formed across her neck from where he grasped her, freezing her breath.

Gasping, she pulled at his hands. His scorched cloak billowed in the air and suddenly she saw it – the Wildwood Arrow – strapped to his chest. She wrenched it free. The Shadow snatched for it and in doing so, he let her fall. Shocked by the sudden plunge, she tried to right herself and only managed to get her wings half open before she smacked into the ground.

Voices sang, high and sweet. The song of the faerie ring seeped into Laney's aching body. The song told a story of fire and water, and underneath it all a voice she thought she recognised called her name. The leaves of the great oak tree shook and the singing faded.

She lay there looking up and a pale figure shot

overhead. The air quivered. Lightning flashed everywhere, cracking open the sky. Bolts of red fought against green, and the green lightning pushed the red back with a shower of sparks. The Shadow blasted more spells through the air but this time the green lightning enveloped the red, folding it up and melting it into nothing. The Shadow wheeled round and flew north, his tattered cloak flying out behind him. The pale figure pursued him, still shooting bolts across the sky, and even without the hat Laney could see that it was Gwen.

She hauled herself up and her voice came out in a croak. "Gwen! I've got the Wildwood Arrow." Then she realised she wasn't holding it. Where was it? She knew she'd had it when she fell. She swayed and everything went blurry.

A hand caught her shoulder. "Maybe you'd better sit down," said Fletcher. "You seem a bit wobbly."

"Fletcher!" She smiled in relief. "You're back to normal."

"Almost." He pulled a leaf out of his hair. "I feel a bit strange – sort of wooden, and my knees and elbows are quite stiff."

Laney checked the ground. "Did you see the Myrical? I took it from the Shadow. I know I was holding it."

"It's here – don't worry." Fletcher picked up the arrow from where it had landed behind the oak tree. "Are you OK? You seem . . . different."

Laney quickly looked down at her hands. The round burn mark on her middle finger stood out against her pale skin like a tiny red moon but the flames in the centre of her palms were gone. What was happening to her? It didn't make any sense.

Fletcher broke the silence. "Thanks for finding a way to bring me back. It shows you're pretty good with magic after all."

"No, I'm not." Laney's throat tightened, thinking of all the struggles she'd had to control her power. "Frogley was right about me and Jessie was right too. I just didn't want to believe them."

"You shouldn't be so hard on yourself. Anyone would find it tough going up against a Shadow faerie."

Claudia limped up to them. "That was the scariest thing ever. But your plan for the potion worked, Laney. Your tribe will have to be proud of you now!"

"You don't understand." Laney realised that they hadn't seen what she'd done. "My powers are all wrong. I'm not a proper Mist faerie."

"Of course you're a Mist. Your dad's a Mist." Fletcher looked at her more closely. "What is it? Did the Shadow hurt you? I couldn't see much while the dark spell was wearing off."

Laney swallowed. She knew she should face the truth but would it mean facing the fact that her own powers were dark too? "When I fought the Shadow just now, something strange happened . . ." She clasped her hands together, feeling the heat rising within. Then she opened her fingers and showed them the tiny golden flames burning in the centre of her palms.

CHAPTER 25

"Laney, what's happened to you?" Fletcher stared at her. "For Thorn's sake, your hands are burning!"

"That's incredible!" Claudia's jaw dropped.

Laney put her hands behind her back. "Don't tell anyone yet. I need some time to figure this out—" She broke off as Gwen flew down and landed beside them.

Gwen closed her pale-green wings. Her eyes had purple smudges beneath them and her skin seemed paper thin, but lightning still sparked at her fingertips. "The Shadow's gone for now, but I never thought to see so much damage." She gazed around at the pitted earth, ripped open by black tree roots.

Laney hesitated. "When we came to your house, you were under a spell. . ."

"The valerian? Yes, I know." Her eyes glinted. "The Shadow should have known that would not hold me for ever. But I never thought to see all this. . ."

"The Shadow poisoned the Wildwood Arrow," Laney told her. "Stingwood started working on a secret project in the forest but he didn't know that the Shadow was using dark magic on the Arrow. As he worked on his Avalon project, he gave himself and the Thorns over to the Shadow's control."

"This still has Shadow magic in it." Fletcher held out the Arrow at arm's length. "I can feel it trying to work on me." His hand trembled and a greenish hue passed across his skin. "And the other Thorns are still bewitched." He indicated the scattered Thorn figures around the park.

Claudia clutched her side where the lightning had struck her. "There's a rain puddle by the swings. I'll dip the arrow in there; if we're lucky it will contain some of the potion we made." She took the Arrow from Fletcher.

"We put moonwort leaves into a bottle of elixir," Laney explained quickly to Gwen. "It was the moonwort you picked at the red moon."

They watched as Claudia dipped the Arrow in the puddle. "Ew!" she said. "All this black gunk is coming out. I think it's safe now. You'd better check it, Fletcher."

"I can't believe I'm letting a Greytail hold the Thorn Myrical," Fletcher said, half to himself. "And I'm actually happy about it."

"There have been strange changes of fortune this day," Gwen said quietly.

Laney remembered her father, injured after fighting the Shadow. "My dad!" she cried. "He's hurt, Gwen. I have to get back to him." And she took off, darting over the great oak tree. Below her, the nearest Thorn statue shook leaves off his body. Mr Thornbeam rubbed his forehead as his skin warmed from greenish-brown back to normal.

Leaving the park behind, she flew over Beacon

Way, where groups of Thorns were standing together and looking confused.

"Gotcha, moss-brain!" Tom Lionhart dived over them, pouring slime over their heads.

"Tom!" Laney called to him. "The Thorns were under a spell but it's broken now."

Tom looked disappointed. The ground rumbled as black roots turned brown and disappeared back into the earth, leaving behind a village overrun with plants and brambles. A gang of hobgobbits advanced down the road in their strange, lurching run, chased by dozens of cats and a horde of crows that dived at them, pecking their hairy bodies. A shaft of sunlight broke through the clouds, showing that the air was clear of the green specks from the valerian spell.

Laney sped up – the humans would soon be waking.

Landing in Oldwing Rise, she changed back to human form and ran home. She pulled thick vines and brambles away from the doorway just as Kim opened the door.

"Laney! Your dad's hurt. I've had to call an ambulance." Kim stared past her stepdaughter. "What on earth! What's happened out here? It's like a wilderness."

Laney hurried inside. Her dad was lying still, eyes closed, the round purple lump on his forehead still visible. His chest rose and fell as he breathed. She knelt down next to him, willing him to wake up. "We have the Wildwood Arrow," she whispered. "The Shadow's gone."

Her dad didn't stir.

"I found him lying here." Kim's face was pale. "I don't know what happened or what he was doing, but he won't wake up."

Laney pressed her lips together. How could she tell Kim that she knew exactly what happened, that she'd seen it? She couldn't tell half the story so it would be better to say nothing at all. She got up and hugged Kim. "I'm sure the ambulance won't be long."

Time passed slowly in the waiting room of Pennington Hospital. Thoughts crowded through Laney's mind as she tried to amuse Toby with books and Lego bricks while Kim talked to a succession of doctors. The ambulance had been slow to arrive as there were still trees lying on parts of the main road. The doctors were performing tests, they were told. It could take a while.

Laney felt as if she couldn't bear it – the long corridors that smelled of disinfectant, the worn-out chairs in the waiting room. She couldn't stop picturing her dad's still face as they'd loaded his stretcher on to the ambulance. He should never have tried to fight the Shadow. Why couldn't she have discovered her fire sooner and used it to help him? She furtively opened her hands. Every time she felt like crying they grew hot again. Quickly she closed them.

As the sun set, the door of the waiting room opened and Claudia and her mum came in. "Kim, I heard about Robert and the nurses said you were in here," said Mrs Lionhart, her quick eyes taking in Kim's tired face. "We came to have Claudia's side looked at. She had an accident on her bike earlier."

Claudia showed them a large bandage over her side. "It doesn't really hurt – looks gross though."

"Oh, dear," said Kim vaguely.

"Laney fly girl!" said Toby, clapping two bricks together.

Laney shushed him.

"Why don't you let us take Laney back to Skellmore with us and she can stay at our house tonight?" said Mrs Lionhart smoothly. "One less thing for you to think about."

"That's very kind." Kim rubbed her neck distractedly. "Then I can take Toby over to my mum's before I come back here to see Robert."

"Exactly." Mrs Lionhart nodded. "Laney, we'll go to your house and you can pick up your things."

Laney hugged Kim and Toby as she left. Then she followed Claudia and her mum back down the long hospital corridor.

"Try not to worry about your dad," said Mrs Lionhart. "We're much quicker to heal than humans – you'll see."

Laney swallowed. "Thanks."

"And by the way, don't be shocked when we get back to Skellmore," Claudia told her. "The place is overrun by more than plants right now."

Laney saw what she meant as they drove up the High Street. Rows of cars and television vans were parked along the side of the road. Cameramen cursed as they tried to unload equipment from the vans, tripping over brambles and cracks in the pavement left by the retreating tree roots.

"I'll drop you here. I'm just going to pick up some things from the shop," Mrs Lionhart said.

Laney and Claudia climbed out, nearly bumping into a woman in a suit talking into her phone. "Careful!" She glared at them.

Claudia scowled back, then she tugged on Laney's arm. "Flippin' heck! Look at that! They're going to interview the Mottles."

Mrs Mottle and Craig stood in front of the hairdresser's next to a serious-looking correspondent. The girls edged nearer to listen.

"And only twelve weeks since they were the centre of a devastating flood, the little village of Skellmore is in the news again," the correspondent said. "In a week when the rest of the country is slipping into autumn, this place has seen huge quantities of plants and flowers literally growing overnight. Residents have had to cut down foliage growing across their doors and windows, and several accidents have been caused by trees obstructing the road." He struck a serious look for the camera.

"Locals are suggesting that this strange phenomenon may be connected to the flood. They say large quantities of fertilisers spread on farmers' fields to help the crops may have entered the water table when those fields were flooded, and this has caused the plants to grow at extraordinary rates. With us now we have Mrs Mottle and her son Craig to explain what happened." He turned to her. "Mrs Mottle, could you tell us what you saw when you got up this morning?"

Mrs Mottle simpered. "It was quite amazing! I said to Craig – didn't I, Craig? – that I'd never seen anything like it. There were plants everywhere. It was very difficult just getting down my front path." She giggled.

"I see," said the correspondent. "Do you think it's strange that this has only happened in Skellmore, leaving the local town unaffected?"

"Ooh, yes," said Mrs Mottle. "This is a very ordinary village and it's always very quiet. So it's a bit of excitement for us!"

"Let's go," groaned Claudia. "I can't stand it." They crossed the High Street, leaving the TV cameras behind. "Do you think people will really believe all that stuff about the fertiliser making the plants go wild? It's such a load of dog biscuits."

Laney shrugged. "What else are they going to believe – that an evil Shadow faerie worked an enchantment over the village? The world they know would collapse if they knew the truth."

"I guess." Claudia kicked a wilting clump of valerian.

"Claudia?" said Laney quietly. "Where's the Wildwood Arrow? Is it safe?"

"Yes." Claudia stopped to let her black cat, Dizzy, wind round her ankles. "Gwen's taken it to Mencladden Hill, ready to put it through the stone at sunrise. She says she can protect it more easily there than in her house." She gave her friend a sideways look.

Laney knew Claudia must be wondering about the flames in her hands and she was grateful to the other girl for not bombarding her with questions.

"You look exhausted," Claudia said at last. "Let's just get your stuff and then we can find something to eat. Unless you want to be interviewed on TV?"

Laney smiled. "I think I'll skip it."

CHAPTER
26

Laney woke up while it was still dark. She was on a blow-up bed on Claudia's floor. The Greytail house growled softly around her, making the floor tremble. She'd got used to it after a while and it had even started to feel comforting. Padding to the window, she looked out at The Cattery, the only street not overrun with plants and brambles. A full moon lit up a cloudless sky and in the park the great oak tree flushed gold as it drew in power from the faerie ring.

Claudia murmured in her sleep and curled up with her knees tucked in. Three cats slept on her bed with her: a large ginger, a tortoiseshell and Dizzy. Seeing her at the window, Dizzy raised her head to watch. Her green eyes looked eerily bright in the dark.

Gwen would be on Mencladden Hill, protecting the arrow ready for sunrise. Laney's mind slid back to the moment when she'd seen the arrow under the Shadow's cloak. He'd had her by the neck, and ice had spread over her skin beneath his grip. She'd hardly been able to breathe. . .

Her hands curled on the windowsill, growing hotter.

Why hadn't she thought of it before?

The Shadow had made ice.

"Claudia!" She shook her friend's shoulder and Dizzy hissed protectively.

"What?" yawned Claudia. "'S too early."

"I'm going to Mencladden Hill now. I'll meet you there, OK?"

"Fine. Whatever." Claudia fell back into her murmuring sleep.

Laney tried to breathe slowly. Her heart was thumping and the little flames had appeared in her hands again. She switched to faerie form, opened Claudia's window and glided into the moonlit night. Dozens of pairs of eyes gazed up at her as she soared over The Cattery. The cats were out in force. She flew over the High Street and skirted round the edge of Hobbin Forest. The Shadow's hold over the arrow was broken but she still felt wary of the trees.

She had to cross Faymere Lake and then the river to reach Mencladden Hill. The full moon cast a broad silver path across the water. Usually she would have swooped low, touching her wing tips against the surface of the water, but today all she could think of was the Shadow's grip on her throat.

She landed at the bottom of the hill, careful not to get too close to the faerie ring that lay near the riverbank. Gwen stood at the top, a faint glow around her winged figure. Towering over her was the ancient Mencladden Stone – a circle with a strange oval hole in the middle. Laney always thought it looked like a giant cat's eye.

"What are you doing here, Laney?" Gwen said as she reached the top. "Sunrise isn't for several hours."

"I've come to tell you: I think the Shadow is a Mist," said Laney breathlessly. "When we were fighting, he took hold of my neck and ice spread across my skin. It must have come from his fingers. We can warn everyone – let them be on the lookout for a Mist faerie."

"Slow down, my dear," said Gwen. "Can you be sure that it was ice and that the Shadow made it?"

"I think so . . . I couldn't see it, but it felt like ice. It all happened so fast." Laney thought of the fight and the Shadow's words. "And there's something else . . . the Shadow said someone had a plan for me. He made it sound as if someone else was in command."

"Someone higher than the Shadow? I had not considered that." Gwen was silent for a minute then she smiled. "Yet so far they have not managed to keep a Myrical. We must maintain our patient, watchful attitude – things have a way of revealing themselves at the right time."

She touched the silvery tip of the Wildwood Arrow and a pulse of magic shot along the wood to the end. "How is your father doing?"

"He's in hospital," Laney told her. "They think he has concussion from hitting his head." A fresh wave of worry rose inside her.

"Try not to be anxious," said Gwen. "I'm sure he just needs time to recover. We are very resilient – much stronger than humans."

"That's what Mrs Lionhart said too."

"Well, we Thorns and Greytails do agree on things from time to time, although it doesn't happen very often." Gwen's wise amber eyes met Laney's. "When he wakes up, I know your father will be very proud of your courage in facing the Shadow. I'm sure your mother would have been proud too, if she was here. Faerie magic is passed down from both parents, you know."

Laney felt a jolt of surprise at the mention of her mum. "But I'm like a disaster area! My powers have gone wrong from the start."

Gwen smiled enigmatically. "Well, your powers did seem weak at first and that's what the Seeing Thread test indicated. But look how magic shines from you now."

Laney glanced at her faerie skin, which glowed with a silvery radiance far brighter than it had a few weeks ago. A tiny suspicion in her mind grew bigger. "Gwen?"

But Gwen stopped her. "Ah! Here are the Thorns. We must prepare."

Laney turned to look. A thin stretch of grey sky on the horizon was steadily growing lighter. It wouldn't be long till sunrise. At the bottom of the hill, dark figures moved into position, forming a ring around the base of the mound. Then slowly they climbed the hill together, stopping close to the top and circling the immense stone.

Laney pressed her hands together to hide the heat inside them. Every single one of them was a Thorn, and they stood waiting in their human form. Nobody spoke, but Laney noticed how tired they looked. Stingwood lurked at the back of the crowd, holding his arms awkwardly as if they still felt wooden. Laney looked round for Fletcher and he gave her a slight smile.

"Thorn friends, welcome!" Gwen's voice rang out. "We await the first light of morning."

Laney gazed at the brightening sky through the hole in the stone and had a vivid memory of putting the Crystal Mirror through that gap, to be locked away inside Time. She remembered how there had been a sudden burst of flame from the top of the stone as she'd done so, and the burn mark on her finger prickled.

Gwen lifted up the Wildwood Arrow. The circle of Thorns didn't move. "This is the Wildwood Arrow, our Thorn Myrical," said Gwen in a clear voice. "We are placing it in the safekeeping of the Mencladden Stone alongside the Crystal Mirror. May the spell hold until we can be free from the danger and fear of the Shadow." A chink of sun appeared in the east, scattering bright rays across the countryside. "From the spring buds and summer flowers, to the autumn leaves and bare winter boughs, we send this Arrow through." And she drove the Arrow into the oval-shaped hole in the centre of the stone where it vanished completely.

A murmur ran round the group of watching Thorns. Mrs Thornbeam wiped her eyes and Mr Thornbeam coughed, while Sara stood between them holding their hands. Laney suddenly felt like she shouldn't be watching, that she was in the middle of something private.

"Friends." Gwen dropped her arms. "Thank you for coming here this morning. I spoke to many of you yesterday but you now know that we have a Shadow faerie in our midst. A few of you have even seen him. I will meet with the Elders of the other tribes as soon as possible to discuss the best course of action."

"Will they all hate us now?" said a little voice, and Sara Thornbeam stepped to the front of the Thorn circle. "There are still brambles everywhere, and it was all our fault."

"No! It was the Shadow – not you!" said Laney. "He poisoned the Arrow with his dark spell. You didn't do anything wrong."

"Some Thorns did," Mr Thornbeam said, his

craggy eyebrows drawing downwards. "Some carried on down the wrong path even though they were warned."

Everyone looked at Stingwood, who met their gaze fiercely. "It's because we're living crammed in with the other tribes and the humans – *that* is the root of the problem. But then you've never seen that, have you? Let's all hold hands with the Greytails and Mists and be nice, that's what you say. We don't know which tribe this Shadow comes from but I'm darned sure he isn't a Thorn."

Laney fidgeted and Gwen gave her a silencing look. "If that's an apology, Peter, it's the worst one I've ever heard," she said crisply. "The truth is that you found the Wildwood Arrow and didn't tell anyone. You put us all in danger by going ahead with your project without the full approval of the tribe."

"Then I apologise." Stingwood leaned on his walking stick to make a mock bow. "I should have known better than to try to build Avalon for you lot." Straightening his massive shoulders, he turned and walked away.

Mrs Thornbeam picked Sara up and smiled at Laney. "Gwen tells us that you and Claudia made the elixir potion that undid the Shadow magic. You should be proud of yourselves. No Thorn could have done better."

"Thanks!" Laney blushed.

"This is for your father, dear." Mr Willowby handed her a tiny cloth bag with some herbs inside. "Rosemary helps speed the healing. Just put it under his pillow."

The Thorns began to leave in small groups, making their way back down the hill. Gwen changed out of faerie form and straightened her blue silk hat. "Claudia! You can come out now."

Claudia appeared from behind a clump of trees and flew up to Laney, Fletcher and Gwen in a graceful glide. "I just didn't want to interrupt all the Thorn stuff."

"But your mum wants you to report back on whether we really did place the arrow in the safety of Mencladden. Isn't that right?" said Gwen. "The Greytails want to be sure."

"She did mention it." Claudia put on a dramatic voice. "*These are dangerous times. We cannot be too careful.* That kind of thing. But I'm glad the tribes finally believe there's a Shadow on the loose now – it'll make things easier."

"What about the Mists?" asked Fletcher. "Do they believe it too? Has anyone seen them?"

"We saw Jessie but she didn't know about the Shadow," said Laney. "My dad said he thought Frogley and the other Mists would send help to Skellmore but I don't think they did."

"Many of them live in Gillforth and Pyton so they may not know the truth of what happened," said Gwen. "But several Thorns saw the Shadow this time so I hope that will overcome any doubts about the matter."

"It is kind of strange," said Claudia thoughtfully. "It's almost as if the Shadow was ready to be seen."

Laney shifted uneasily, looking at Gwen. "Can I tell them what I think?"

"Tell us what?" said Claudia, wide-eyed.

"Tell them but be sure not to share this with anyone else. As yet this is only a suspicion, and a wrongful accusation could cause immense damage to relations between the tribes. You heard what Stingwood said – already people are starting to draw their own conclusions," Gwen said seriously. "I must go now. There's much to be done to get Skellmore back to rights – vines to untangle and thickets to banish. I hope those wretched TV people don't get in my way!" She hobbled steadily down the hill.

"Well, Laney?" Claudia looked like her eyes would pop. "Tell us *what*?"

"I think maybe the Shadow came from the Mist tribe. He used ice when we were fighting and how could he have done that if he wasn't a Mist?" said Laney.

Claudia looked shocked. "A Mist! I didn't think

any of them were that powerful. No offence!"

"It all happened fast," said Laney, "so it's hard to be completely sure."

"Then we shouldn't jump to conclusions about who he is yet." Fletcher's eyebrows lowered and for a moment he looked exactly like his dad. "But one day we'll know. I want to see this monster defeated after what he did to my tribe."

Laney hadn't heard him talk like that before. "I think I have something else to tell you as well but . . ." She hesitated. "I need to be sure that I'm right first. I'll meet you at the bridge over the river in a couple of hours."

Fletcher looked concerned. "Do you need any help?"

"No, I'm fine," Laney insisted. "I'll meet you there, OK?"

"Mysterious! But you know you can't keep a secret from us for long!" Claudia spread her wings.

"Let's go, Miss Curiosity!" Fletcher spread his wings too, and he and Claudia flew away.

Laney walked down the empty hill, slowing as she reached the bottom. The reeds at the river's edge moved and a duck emerged, flapping its wings. Diamond flecks danced on the water in the light of the rising sun.

Between Laney and the river lay the faerie ring with its secrets.

You can't keep a secret from us for long, Claudia had said.

Maybe that was true. How could anyone bear to keep a secret for a long time? But if her suspicions were right that's exactly what her dad had been doing.

She made herself take a tiny step forwards, and another and another, until she could hear the high voices inside the faerie ring. Their song started up faintly, telling of life, death and magic, and the Otherworld beyond. She felt the familiar pulling sensation, the urge to get closer and hear more. At the same time knowing that if she took a step too close it would be the last thing she ever did.

Then she heard what she was really listening for – a voice she thought she knew. She sank to her knees. "Mum?"

The voice carried on speaking softly with no sign that it had heard her. Was it her mum? And if she spoke did sounds pass the other way through the ring? Laney leaned closer. The voice was telling a story of fire and water. She knelt there listening until the other voices grew louder, drowning out everything else with their song.

CHAPTER
27

Pulling herself away from the ring, Laney unfolded her wings and flew along the riverbank until she got closer to Skellmore. Then she ran the rest of the way back to Oldwing Rise. The house was horribly quiet and empty, with half a cup of tea standing on the side in the kitchen and Toby's toys strewn across the sitting room. She felt a twinge of sadness at being away from Kim and Toby, especially while her dad was hurt. She would ask Claudia's mum to drive her back to Pennington Hospital in a little while but before that there was something she had to know.

She went to the bookcase and took down the blue shoebox with her birth certificate and the old photos inside. She took out the birth certificate and read the date: *15th July*. Then she looked at the line below with her mum's name, *Cordelia*, and the smudged surname next to it. Her dad had told her for years that her mum had been called Cordelia Brightsea. But now that she looked closely, the barely decipherable capital letter of the second name didn't look like a B. It looked more like an E.

She stared at it until her eyes started to go fuzzy. There was something strange about all this – the smudge over the surname and the way her dad had never wanted to talk about marrying her mum. Surely he'd kept something that would tell her more. She searched through the whole shoebox but it was all receipts and gas bills in her dad's name. Running upstairs, she went into her dad and Kim's room. Feeling guilty, she rifled through drawer after drawer. There was nothing, just clothes and an old book at the bottom of her dad's bedside table. She pulled it out. It had a picture of a couple of animals in a rowing boat on the front. Why was he keeping a copy of *The Wind in the Willows* in his bedside drawer? She picked it up and a tattered bookmark fell out. She flicked backwards through the yellowing pages till she came to the front.

There was a name in the inside cover, written in round, childish handwriting: *Cordelia Embers*. This had been her mum's book.

Embers. It had to be a Blaze tribe name.

Laney sat down on the bed, holding the book tightly. Her mum had belonged to the tribe with power over fire. Her dad hadn't married another Mist faerie after all.

She traced a finger over the name Embers. If her mum had been a Blaze faerie then what did that make her? She'd been so sure that she was a Mist and her dad must have believed that too. He must have thought she'd inherited his Mist powers rather than her mum's Blaze ones. He'd always refused to have any fire in the house – no candles, no matches, nothing. Was it because fire reminded him too much of losing her mum? Or had he wanted to make sure any traces of Blaze power stayed hidden deep inside her?

Taking the book with her, she went downstairs and tidied up all the papers and her birth certificate back into the shoebox. Before putting the box away, she took out her favourite photo – the one of her mum standing in the bare, windswept garden holding her as a baby. She slipped the picture inside the front cover of *The Wind in the Willows* and hid the book at the bottom of the shoebox.

Closing her eyes, she switched to faerie form and felt a new sense of warmth underneath the rush of power. She looked into the mirror above the mantelpiece. Her eyes were gold-ringed and a blue dress clothed her faerie form as it always had. But her wings . . . she flexed them and her throat tightened. Her pale-blue wings were tinged with flame-like orange all around the edges. The coppery tint caught the light as she flexed them.

She'd changed and instinctively she knew there was no going back.

Her hands grew hot and she opened her fingers to release the little flames that danced in the centre of her palms. It wasn't a safe kind of power, this Blaze magic, but it was hers and having it made her feel stronger.

Fletcher and Claudia were waiting for her on the

bridge sharing a big bag of toffee popcorn.

"Guess what!" Claudia smoothed her dark hair. "My mum's gone off to meet the other Elders for a War Council about the Shadow. I bet they don't even thank us for finding out about him in the first place."

"It doesn't really matter as long as they catch him," said Fletcher calmly.

"It won't be easy," said Laney. "The Shadow won't give up. He knows the tribes will argue with each other and he'll be ready to use that against them."

"You're very wise all of a sudden!" Claudia scrutinised Laney. "Are you ready to reveal your Grand Secret now?"

Laney's stomach lurched; suddenly she felt worried about what they might think. "Don't be shocked, but it's kind of unusual." She took a deep breath.

"Is it about that prophecy and how you Awakened on the night of that red moon?" said Claudia. "That was my guess. You've found something out about the prophecy – how does it go? Something about breaking a faerie ring and a child of fever?"

"Child of Aether," corrected Fletcher. "Although I don't know what that means."

"No, it's nothing to do with that." Laney dragged her fingers through her fair hair. "You're making it harder."

"Sorry!" Claudia clamped her lips shut and fixed her cat-like eyes on Laney.

Laney took another deep breath but she couldn't think of the right thing to say so she just held out her hands. The flames from her palms leapt high, full of golden heat. "I think my mum was really a Blaze faerie. Her surname was actually Embers. I found it written inside an old book. She must have passed her Blaze power on to me."

Claudia's eyes grew round. "A Blaze! Well, that explains *a lot*! And your dad never said anything about it?"

"He told me her surname was Brightsea – a Mist name," Laney admitted.

"I've heard of people marrying someone from another tribe and getting into huge amounts of trouble," said Fletcher. "Maybe that's why he didn't tell you."

Laney said quickly. "This is just between us. I can't ask my dad any more till he's better so I'd rather not tell the Elders."

"No wonder the Mist training didn't go well." Fletcher shook his head. "Don't worry, I won't say anything to anybody."

Laney flushed with relief. "I know it's all been weird – with my powers and stuff. . ."

"Relax!" Claudia grinned. "I guess I'd better stop calling you Water Girl now. Flame Girl suits you better anyway."

"I just thought I should tell you." Laney closed her hands again. "I ought to go back. I need to visit my dad at the hospital." She turned back across the bridge with the others by her side.

"So the flames in your hands don't hurt then?" Claudia asked curiously. "And could you throw one at an enemy – like a fireball? Or could you point at something and make it melt? Or—"

"Leave her be," said Fletcher. "She doesn't know yet."

Laney grinned. "I'm not ready to show off any fire skills yet. But when I am you'll be the first to know." She felt warmth pulsing in the palms of her hands and her heart rose. There was so much more to find out about being a Blaze. She'd only just begun.

Acknowledgements

Thanks to everyone at Nosy Crow for being tirelessly supportive and for believing in me. A special thanks to Kirsty who patiently pushed me to the next level and was insightful and wise.

A big thanks to my writing group, including Nick Cross, Penny Schenk, Nicki Thornton and Jo Wyton for reading endless variations of the first chapter. Particular thanks to Amy Butler Greenfield and Sally Poyton who read the whole thing. Also thanks to Teri Terry for being there. There have been many people in SCBWI who offered friendship and encouragement along the way. You all helped me on the days where it seemed there was so far to travel.

Thanks to my mum and dad, and my sister, whose enthusiasm has given me such a boost. Thanks to my children for sharing this with me and for keeping my feet on the ground. Most of all, thanks to James for being prepared to live with someone who doesn't realise that dinner needs cooking, and who walks into the kitchen and starts a conversation with: "Well, if Laney doesn't realise until it's too late then everything will reach a climax in the next chapter..."